# BATMAN

WARNER BROS. Presents

JACK NICHOLSON    MICHAEL KEATON    KIM BASINGER

A GUBER–PETERS COMPANY Production A TIM BURTON Film "BATMAN" ROBERT WUHL

PAT HINGLE    BILLY DEE WILLIAMS    MICHAEL GOUGH and JACK PALANCE Songs by PRINCE

Music Score by DANNY ELFMAN Executive Producers BENJAMIN MELNIKER and MICHAEL USLAN

Co-Producer CHRIS KENNEY Based upon Batman Characters Created by BOB KANE Published by DC COMICS

Story by SAM HAMM Screenplay by SAM HAMM and WARREN SKAAREN Produced by JON PETERS & PETER GUBER

TM & © 1989 DC Comics Inc.              Directed by TIM BURTON

 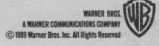

# BATMAN

Novelization by **CRAIG SHAW GARDNER**

Based on the Story by **SAM HAMM** and

The Screenplay by **SAM HAMM & WARREN SKAAREN**

And the Character Created by **BOB KANE**

WARNER BOOKS

A Warner Communications Company

WARNER BOOKS EDITION

Copyright © 1989 by DC Comics, Inc.
All rights reserved.

Warner Books, Inc.
666 Fifth Avenue
New York, N.Y. 10103

 A Warner Communications Company

Printed in the United States of America

First Printing: June, 1989

10 9 8 7 6

This one's for
THE MILLION YEAR PICNIC
and all who toil and buy therein.

# Prologue

It was a night like any other in the city—too hot, too humid, too loud. The sound of music mixed with car horns and laughter and the occasional scream. The streets swarmed with life, ten times as busy now that the sun was gone and the scum of the night could crawl from their holes, like roaches who needed the darkness to feed.

Not that the streets were dark. Some of the streetlights still worked, enough to show the pushers wave to the hookers, the hustlers laughing as some sucker got fleeced at three-card monte, the addicts and alkies huddled in their corners, at peace as long as their stash held out. Brighter still were the tattoo parlors, the peep shows, the broken-down saloons—the unwashed windows swarming with their neon imitations of daylight. And over it all, Luna, the full moon, ancient symbol of madness, rose to show its approval.

Welcome to Gotham City.

It was the city at night, full of lost souls and street trash that most places hide in the shadows, sweep in the gutters. But Gotham was too big, too out of control: Here, the hookers and pushers and hustlers and addicts were all on a first-name basis; here, the shadows and the gutters had taken over.

Here, everybody knew the rules. It was one big, happy family—unless you were from outside.

A mother, a father, and a twelve-year-old son, little Jimmy, all too well dressed for this kind of neighborhood, walked down the festering street, out-of-towners trying not to look out of place, which marked them even more. They carried playbills in their hands. They'd just been to a show, but had walked the wrong way and left the theater crowd far behind.

A group of strangers looked them up and down, smiling as they hurried by. A wino staggered in their path. Mother clutched at father's sleeve.

"For God's sake, Harold, can we please just get a taxi?"

Harold looked back at his wife with an annoyed, even angry expression, the kind of look that would make him king of the household back wherever they came from.

"I'm trying to get a—" He raised both arms and waved as he shouted, *"Taxi!"*

One cab sped by, followed by two more. Nobody wanted to stop in this neighborhood.

Little Jimmy reached in his back pocket and pulled out a map. He frowned as he started to unfold it.

"We're going the wrong way."

Behind them, some of the strangers were starting to snicker.

"Put that away!" the father insisted, trying to keep his voice low, trying not to attract attention. "We'll look like tourists."

He led his family toward a pair of cops leaning against a patrol car outside of an all-night souvlaki stand. The cops were too busy chatting and laughing with a fourteen-year-old hooker to pay them much attention. The hooker glanced around and smiled at little Jimmy. Little Jimmy smiled back.

His mother yanked him violently away. She glowered at her husband. It looked as if there was going to be a fight.

"We'll never get a cab," Harold admitted. "Let's cut over to Seventh."

Their son stopped as they turned the corner. Little Jimmy pointed behind them.

"Seventh is *that* way!"

"I know where we are!" his father announced as he marched into darkness. On this street—not much more than an alley, really—the lights were gone. His wife and son followed, all three walking quickly around the derelict cars, lit only by the glare of the swollen moon.

"Hey, mister!" a voice called out of the darkness. "Gimme a dollar?"

A man sat against one of the wrecks. He was maybe nineteen or twenty, his face pocked with acne scars. His torn T-shirt read "I Love Gotham City."

Father hurried his family along, as if none of them had heard.

"Mister!" the guy who loved Gotham City yelled. "How about it? One dollar?" He lurched to his feet, his voice even louder. "Are you deaf? Do you speak English?"

The family walked quickly to the far side of the alley. The derelict only stood and watched them, swaying back and forth, pushed by a wind that wasn't there. The father barely stopped himself from glancing behind, to see if they were safe. He didn't notice the other figure hiding in the shadows, the one with the gun. The gun that came down quickly, brutally, across the father's neck.

Father fell. Mother grabbed little Jimmy. They backed up against a rough brick wall, too scared to make a sound. The guy who loved Gotham City ran across the street to join his friend with the gun, the friend who was already ripping through father's pockets to see what he could find. Mother made a mewling noise, deep in her throat. The friend paused in his task and pointed the gun straight at little Jimmy.

"Do the kid a favor, lady," he said softly and reasonably. "Don't scream."

She swallowed her scream instead. Tears streamed down her face. She held little Jimmy tight against her, as if her son was the only thing that was keeping her sane. Little Jimmy didn't say anything either, as if all he could think about was the muzzle of a gun.

The two friends found what they wanted. They chuckled as they ran away.

Mother stared at her husband, crumpled in the alleyway. He was totally still. She wasn't even sure if he was breathing.

She couldn't help herself anymore.

She started to scream.

Welcome to Gotham City.

The scream echoed up and down the alleyway. It mixed with the music, and the laughter, and the car horns down on the street. It rose up past the derelict cars and worn brick walls to sweep through the towers of the old City Cathedral, once the spiritual center of a great metropolis, now fallen into ruin itself. Stone gargoyles watched from the cathedral towers, monsters carved in the walls of the church—so tradition had it—to keep the evil spirits away. But these gargoyles only watched the evil and listened to the screams.

Until one of the gargoyles moved.

Welcome to Gotham City.

The friends—"I Love Gotham City" and the one with the gun; let's call them Nick and Eddie, now—ran all the way to a safe place, a roof, six stories above the street, to take a look at what they'd found. Nick opened up the wallet and started looking at the cards.

"All right! American Express." He tossed the card at Eddie. "Don't leave home without it, heh?"

He turned his attention to counting the cash.

The night wind picked up, blowing gravel across the roof. Eddie looked up. He had heard a noise, like metal clanging against metal.

He looked over at Nick.

"Let's beat it, man. I don't like it up here."

Nick laughed. "What are ya, scared of heights?"

"I dunno." Eddie couldn't help looking around, even though there was nothing out there except the darkness. "After what happened to Johnny Gobs—"

That made Nick angry. "Look, Johnny Gobs got ripped and walked off a roof, all right? No big loss."

But Eddie knew it wasn't that simple. "No, man. That ain't what I heard at all." He stopped for a minute, as if he didn't want to say what came next. But it had to come out.

"I heard the bat got him."

"The *bat*?" Nick looked away, as if his friend's idea wasn't even worth laughing about. "Gimme a break, will you, Eddie?"

But Eddie shook his head. "Five stories, straight down. There was no blood in the body."

"No shit," Nick agreed. "It was all over the pavement." His head whipped around. He stared out into the dark. This time, he had heard the sound.

He looked back at Eddie.

"Shut up!" he barked. "Listen to me. There ain't no bat."

All of Eddie was shaking now. "You shouldn'ta turned the gun on that kid, man. You shouldn'ta—"

"You want your cut of this money or don't you?" Nick was yelling now. "Now, shut up! *Shut up*—"

He stopped when he heard the new sound. It was different this time, and closer, and they both knew what it was—boots crunching on gravel.

They both turned to look. Eddie made a strangled, gurgling sound. Something darker than the night stood on the edge of the roof. It walked toward them. Maybe it was a man. It spread what should have been its arms slowly, majestically. There was movement below those arms, like a shadow of something that wasn't there, or a great pair of leathery wings. On its chest there was a yellow oval that seemed to glow with a light of its own. And in the middle of that oval was the deep black emblem of a bat.

Nick pulled out his gun and dropped to the gravel. He fired twice at the bat emblem, two clean shots. He was too close to miss. The black figure jerked back as they hit, then fell to the roof with a satisfyingly solid sound.

"I'm gettin' out of here," Nick whispered. He turned around to grab the wallet.

Eddie made a low noise, too scared to scream. Nick looked back. The human bat was standing again, and it was coming for them.

The money fell out of Nick's fingers and fluttered away on the night breeze. He had to get out of this place! Nick kept low, half running, half crawling across the roof. There was someone blocking the way, someone standing in front of the fire escape. A human bat.

No one was going to trap him like this! Nick fired again and again and again, the gun shaking in his hand.

This time, the bullets didn't do anything at all. The bat walked forward. Eddie was in its path, huddled on the roof, unable to do anything except piss in his pants. The bat walked around him. As the thing passed, a single black boot caught Eddie in the middle of the chest. It lifted him completely off his feet and sent him flying through the air into a brick chimney. Eddie slumped to the roof, out cold.

And the bat didn't even stop. It just kept on walking.

Nick had to get away. He jumped up, fear moving his legs, and ran past the moving shadow, toward the fire escape and—

The bat moved its hand, as if it was throwing something.

Nick was falling forward. He could no longer use his legs. They were pinned together, wrapped in something, rope or wire. Nick screamed. He had to get away. His arms were still free. He pulled his body along the rooftop, the gravel slicing into his elbows, drawing a dozen tiny streams of blood. Nick couldn't think about the pain. He could think only about the bat.

He dragged himself to the edge of the roof. The bat stayed right behind him, never overtaking him but never far away. There was no place for Nick to go. No place he could escape. There was only the ledge, and the bat.

Nick almost lost it, almost crapped in his pants like that candy-ass Eddie, until he remembered the gun. No one could get him when he had the gun. Both his hands shook as he lifted his piece, so much heavier than it was before. He shot and shot again, but he could no longer open his eyes to aim.

*Click.* The hammer hit an empty chamber.

*Click. Click. Click.*

Something came from inside Nick, a hopeless sound. The sound of somebody who was about to die.

He felt two hands grab his shirt and lift him from the roof.

"Don't kill me," Nick whispered. "Don't kill me."

Nick opened his eyes. The bat stood on the edge of the roof, and he held Nick out beyond the edge, over nothing.

The bat opened his mouth. His voice was a rasp, like a file biting into steel.

"You're trespassing, rat-breath."

Nick looked down—six stories down, at the tiny, tiny cars so far below. He looked up into the bat's face, but where the thing's eyes should have been were two mirrors, twin reflections of Nick's fear.

Nick tried to ignore the pounding in his ears, the feeling of his legs kicking out at nothing but air. What did it matter? He was going to die anyway. He'd tell off the bat before he went.

"Trespassing?" He tried to laugh, but it came out as more of a cough. "You don't own the night."

The bat smiled.

"Tell your friends. Tell all your friends." The smile widened to show teeth. "I am the night."

Nick screamed as he felt the bat's grip on him shift. He was spun around and thrown roughly on the tar-and-gravel rooftop. He still managed to look up, to see the bat step off the building's edge, six stories up, off into nothing but air.

What was going on? Nick couldn't help himself. He had to see where the bat had gone. He crawled to the ledge and looked over, six stories down.

There was no one there. The bat had disappeared.

That's when Nick really started to scream.

Welcome to Gotham City, punk.

A new Gotham City.

# C H A P T E R

## One

Commissioner Gordon looked out over the crowd. The large hall at the Gotham City Democrats Club was packed. The huge victory banner said it all:

CONGRATULATIONS!
A NEW GOTHAM CITY!
HARVEY DENT—DISTRICT ATTORNEY

At least the banner described Gordon's dreams. A new Gotham City? Gordon hoped, somehow, that Dent could make a difference. But he had seen others like Dent before him—bright, idealistic, full of fervor to reform that beast they called Gotham City.

Most of the time, the beast got the reformer, not the other way around. There were too many people here, too many ins and outs, too many temptations, too much politics. Gordon's own hands weren't as clean as he wished they could be. But he was still here, a survivor, and with luck he could still do some good.

He turned his head to look up and down the head table. It seemed that every reform-minded dignitary in the whole city was here; Brown, Estevez, O'Neil, Cleveland. At least, all the reformers were *supposed* to be here. Gordon noted that the chair two down from the speaker, the one reserved for Bruce Wayne, was vacant. Gordon was a little surprised by that. Wayne had worked as hard as anybody here to get Dent elected.

For all that the newspapers went on about "millionaire playboy Bruce Wayne," he was actually very dependable, very committed. If they could get a few more millionaire playboys with Wayne's resources working for Gotham, they could turn the city around in no time. Wayne must have had a good reason for staying away. Maybe, Gordon thought as he looked regretfully down at the gray remains on his plate, he couldn't face up to any more meals of rubber roast beef.

Gordon looked up again, his old politician's face graced with the hint of a smile. He had learned, through years of public service, to keep as pleasant an expression on his face as possible, no matter what they were having for dinner. Besides, there might be a reason to smile after all.

Dent had won in a landslide over the incumbent, a fellow whom the voters finally realized had been living in the pocket of the mob for the past twenty years. Maybe the vote meant that Gordon and the city had enough people behind them this time to make a difference. Maybe truth and justice would triumph for a change, and some of the real criminals would end up behind bars.

Maybe this, maybe that. Gordon sighed as he glanced to his left. There were few things certain in this world, but one of them was that he would always have to attend these political dinners, and, at every one of them, his honor, the mayor, would make a speech.

Mayor Borg stood, proud as an overstuffed peacock, as if Dent's election was somehow all his doing. Gordon knew that the mayor was only supposed to introduce Dent, a job that, in Borg's hands, could take a good twenty minutes.

The crowd quieted as Borg started to speak. Gordon only half listened. Heaven knew, Borg sounded as if he never even listened to himself. The mayor went on about "our fair city" and "this great flower of the east." He thanked his constituents, most of them, seemingly, by name. Only then did Borg start something that could lead to an introduction. Gordon finally decided to give the mayor his full attention.

Borg took a deep breath, a gesture that should have been dramatic but instead hinted at a life of too many cigarettes. "Across this nation," he spoke again, "the words 'Gotham City' are synonymous with crime. Our streets are overrun, and our police officials have been helpless. As mayor, I promised you that I would root out the source of corruption at the root!" He paused for another breath, raising a pudgy forefinger skyward. "Boss Carl Grissom! Our new district attorney, Harvey Dent, will carry out on that promise. I promise!"

Harvey Dent stood, and the audience was on their feet as well, clapping and cheering. This part of Gotham City really was ready for a change.

Dent motioned for quiet, and a moment later the audience agreed, returning to their seats so that they could hear the new district attorney speak.

Tall and thin, he looked as though he had been born in a business suit. His deep-brown skin gleamed under the lights. Gordon realized that that was another thing to be thankful for. Dent's leading-man looks would go over well on television—a lot better than a middle-aged, sagging, overweight police commissioner.

Dent started to speak, his voice so clear he hardly needed the microphone. "I'm a man of few words. But those words will count. And so will our actions. I have talked today to Police Commissioner Gordon."

There was a smattering of applause. For the police commissioner? Gordon smiled politely. My, he thought, the audience was being generous tonight.

"He is targeting businesses," Dent continued, "suspected of fronting for the syndicate in this city. Within one week, we'll knock down their doors—" He paused, his eyes sweeping the crowd. "—and shed the light of the law on that nest of vipers!"

There was real applause this time. Gordon wished he could enjoy it more. He had a real job in front of him this time. A job that entailed a lot more than sitting around at fancy dress dinners. Most of the time, as long as you did what you were supposed to, the public managed to ignore the police commissioner. All this attention was making Gordon a little uncomfortable.

Damn! Sometimes he wished he had the freedom to play hooky like Wayne. He could already tell that the rubber roast beef was going to give him gas. He smiled politely at Dent, and hoped his stomach would stay quiet long enough for the new D.A. to outline the rest of their plan —a plan that Gordon hoped, somehow, against all the odds, they could turn into a reality.

What a dump!

Jack Napier absently fiddled with his lucky deck. It was amazing, with all the money Alicia Hunt had—not only from her modeling career, but from all those little presents Boss Grissom always gave her—that she could have filled her apartment up with such crap. What was this liver-shaped coffee table, anyway, post-Yugoslavian modern or something? Others might call it classy, but to him it was just expensive junk. At least it gave him a place to rest his feet. And the way she covered the walls with her modeling pictures—well, at least it covered the walls.

Jack chuckled at his own private joke. Since she slept with him, she had to have excellent taste in men. Too bad she didn't have taste in anything else.

Jack finished his one-handed shuffle. He turned his attention back to the television and this stiff who had just gotten himself elected.

Who exactly was this guy? The newswoman had said his name only a minute ago. Bend? Bent? Dent—that was it. Not that there was anything particularly new about him. He spoke like any other politician Jack had ever heard. Jack had to admit, however, that the guy looked classy.

Napier dealt four jacks off the top of the deck, each card with a bullet hole in its center.

"Together we can make this city safe for decent people," Dent droned on.

"Decent people shouldn't live here," Jack said back to the set. "They'd be happier someplace else."

Alicia glided across the room. She might not have any taste, but she still looked pretty good, especially in that skimpy black negligee. She lifted his feet and rescued a *Vogue* magazine with her picture on the cover. Imagine that, Jack thought. He had been resting his Italian shoes on her face. He noticed with a frown that one of the polished black toes had a slight scuff. He'd have to fix that.

Alicia brushed at her straight blond hair as she stared at the television.

"Pretty tough talk about Carl."

Jack waved away her observation with a flick of his lucky deck.

"Don't worry about it. If this clown could touch Grissom, I'd have killed him by now."

Alicia leaned down over Jack, revealing even more of her cleavage. She grabbed his loosely knotted tie and pulled it tightly around his neck.

"If Grissom knew about us," she mentioned, "he might kill *you*."

Jack glanced from the TV over to a mirror above a nearby vanity. Damn, but that tie looked good on him! At least he had good taste—impeccable taste, really. He smiled at his reflection. He might try to give Alicia lessons, but you were either born with this or you never got it.

"Don't flatter yourself, angel," he murmured, glancing at her at last. "He's a tired old man. He can't run this city without me." He looked at himself in the mirror one more time. "And besides, he doesn't know."

He flipped the TV off with the remote.

Alicia frowned at him as he stood. "You don't worry about anything, do you, Jack?"

Jack smiled to prove exactly how worried he was. He glanced at his watch. Time to go. He grabbed his topcoat from the couch and stood in front of the vanity to put it on. He smoothed down the dark cashmere, checked to make sure his hair was in place. Yeah. Nothing but the best for old Jack.

"You look fine," she reassured him.

Jack smiled at his reflection.

"I didn't ask."

The reflection smiled back.


Alexander Knox tried not to even breathe too loudly.

He had been rushing down the alley, anxious to get to the scene of the crime. That was before he heard Lieutenant Eckhardt talking to the police medic around the corner. That's right, Eckhardt actually talking! The minute Knox showed up, the chubby officer always became dumber than one of the Three Stooges.

Sometimes, Knox considered, you could be the best damn newspaper reporter in all of Gotham City by just taking an extra minute to get there.

"You know what that guy says he saw . . ." the medic began incredulously.

"No, let me guess," Eckhardt wheezed. "A gigantic, menacing, supernatural form—in the shape of a bat?"

"That's it!" was the other man's astonished reply. "What are they seeing up there?"

Eckhardt dismissed it. "They're all drinkin' Drano."

"It's still weird, Lieutenant," the medic allowed.

"Oh, Christ," Eckhardt muttered in a half-whisper. "Knox!"

Whoops. Knox had gotten a little too interested and a little too far out into the alley. Well, now that his cover was blown, he might as well make the best of it. He stepped toward Eckhardt with a big grin.

"Hiya, gents. I hear we got another bat attack." Eckhardt winced. Knox's smile got even wider. "That's eight sightings now in just under a month. I even hear the commissioner's opened a file."

"Sorry, Knox," Eckhardt replied, his face as expressive as your average slab of granite. "Those two slipped on a banana peel."

Two? So there were two crooks involved? Sometimes Eckhardt gave away tidbits without even knowing it. Knox wondered if there was any way he could sneak in a question or two with the eyewitnesses.

That's when one of the eyewitnesses got dragged past by a pair of cops. For a minute, Knox thought that Eckhardt might be right. This guy sure looked as though he could have been drinking Drano. What clothes he had left were torn in half a dozen places, the skin beneath crisscrossed with the dull brown of drying blood. His hair was matted with blood, too, but what was really weird was the guy's face. He was smiling.

"A bat, I tell you, a giant bat!" He giggled and twitched, his head jerking from Eckhardt to Knox to each of his captors. "He wanted me to do him a favor."

The cops dragged him away before the favor could be

performed. Knox grinned at Eckhardt anyway. His most important question had been answered.

Eckhardt actually let his irritation show. "Don't be writing this crap in the newspaper, Knox. It'll ruin your already useless reputation."

But Knox had this fat bastard now. An eyewitness to the bat!

He pressed his advantage. "Lieutenant, lots of punks in town are scared stiff! They say he drinks blood. They say he can't be killed!"

"I say you're full of shit, Knox," Eckhardt barked as he turned away. "And you can quote me on that!"

So, they were going to stonewall him, even now? Knox couldn't give up that easily.

"Lieutenant. Is there a six-foot bat in Gotham City?"

Eckhardt walked away without looking back.

Knox shouted after him, "If so, is he on the police payroll?"

Eckhardt lumbered around the corner, out of sight.

"If so," Knox persisted, "what's he pulling down after taxes?"

There was no answer. Knox hadn't really expected one. He thought for a second about following the lieutenant, but decided it would be better for his health and career if he didn't. As much as Knox disliked the guy, it didn't pay to be too annoying.

Besides, he had gotten what he really wanted. Fried or not, that smiling guy had seen the human bat. And Knox found it even more fascinating that, for some reason, the police didn't want the story getting out. Eckhardt and the others should know by now that that sort of attitude just made Allie Knox want the truth that much more.

Who was this guy who tried to look like a bat, of all things? A renegade cop? A criminal? Some kind of a vigilante? Or a total nut case? Knox had a feeling he might be every one of the above. And he was going to find out, and report everything he found in the *Gotham Globe*.

When he was done, the human bat was going to be better known than Pee Wee Herman. And whatever the police were covering up would be splashed across the front page.

# C H A P T E R
## Two

Ah, here was the slob now. He looked nervously up and down the street as he waddled toward them. Gotham City's finest, unshaven, his flab quivering up and down under his too-tight suit, threatening to burst his buttons with every step he took. Why couldn't Eckhardt take better care of himself?

Jack Napier leaned back on the hood of the stretch limo. Bob Hawkins, his right-hand man and insurance policy, was doing the usual—straightening the mirror, polishing the door handle—busy, but available, should the situation arise.

Jack pushed himself upright and tossed the lieutenant a sandwich bag.

"I brought you a little snack, Eckhardt."

The cop opened the bag to look suspiciously at the sandwich. The bread was stuffed with hundred-dollar bills.

The cop looked back down the street where he came from as he tucked the sandwich in his coat.

"Why don't you broadcast it, Napier?" The lieutenant seemed a little irritated. Must have gotten up on the wrong side of the bed. But that was no reason to get uppity with Jack. Napier decided it was time to put Grissom's toady in his place.

"Shut up and listen," Jack ordered. "Harvey Dent is sniffing around one of our companies."

That managed to make the lieutenant even more steamed.

"That's my territory, Jack," he snapped as he marched toward the limo. "If there's a problem—"

Jack had had enough from fat boy. His hands snaked out to grab Eckhardt's coat.

"Eckhardt," he said simply, directly. "Your problems are our problems."

The cop knocked Jack's hands away. "I answer to Grissom, not to psychos!"

"Why, Eckhardt," Jack replied with the slightest hint of surprise. "You should be thinking about the future."

"You mean"—the cop sneered—"when you run the show?" He waved his pudgy hand in dismissal. "You got no future, Jack. You're an A-one nut boy, and Grissom knows it!"

Jack clapped a hand to Eckhardt's overfed face. He pivoted around, pushing the cop hard against the brick wall at the alley's side. Eckhardt blinked, stunned by the suddenness of the move. Jack almost felt sorry for a second. But, after all, fat boy had so much padding, he shouldn't have felt a thing.

Eckhardt's face had turned the same color Santa Claus usually wore. He grabbed Jack's coat collar and whipped out his police special.

Jack took his hand away as Eckhardt brought up his gun. Jack glanced at the gun, then the fat fingers on his collar.

"Watch the suit," he remarked casually.

Eckhardt was having trouble catching his breath. He frowned at Napier, then let go of the coat and lowered the gun.

Jack smiled. What a good fat boy.

"See?" he added pleasantly. "You can make a good decision when you really, really try."

Jack started to laugh. All the color drained from Eckhardt's face. That only made Jack laugh harder. Boy, the fat boy was really boiling now! Jack strolled back to where Bob had just opened the rear door of the limo. Jack couldn't watch the cop anymore. Tears were streaming down his face. He glanced back a final time as he got in the car.

Something almost stopped Jack's mirth.

When he looked back, why was Eckhardt smiling? Jack dismissed it, unable to hear Eckhardt having the last word, muttering "And where have you been spending your nights, handsome."


The red, yellow, and black banner flapped in the early-autumn wind: "200TH ANNIVERSARY OF GOTHAM CITY FESTIVAL."

Borg waved impatiently for Dent and Gordon to follow. The mayor could be surprisingly energetic when he was motivated, and he was taking this big anniversary celebration personally. They had already visited one of the float manufacturers and the Gotham Uniform Supply Company, personally making sure everything would be ready for the big day. Now the mayor was dragging them along to personally inspect the final construction of the reviewing stand in Gotham Square.

Gordon felt as though they had been trudging around for hours. Today, he thought, Dent was really going to find out what it was like working for Gotham City.

"I don't care how much in debt this festival is!" the mayor shouted back at them as he bustled along. "I want a parade, hot dogs, balloons, the whole schmeer. We're gonna celebrate this two hundredth anniversary proudly. And *publicly*!"

Somehow, Dent was trying to remain the voice of reason in the face of all this.

"We may be celebrating it in bankruptcy court," he gently reminded the mayor. "The tax base is crumbling, and if this festival crashes you can kiss your bond rating good-bye. This festival is three hundred and fifty thousand in the red, and we haven't seen one balloon."

"I'll take care of the festival budget!" the mayor insisted, his voice rising again. Gordon sometimes thought the mayor was sure, if he was only loud enough, he could outshout whatever logic was thrown against him.

"I've got a party of rich old ladies who'll pay a thousand dollars each to see the the inside of Wayne Manor!" the mayor blustered along. "You fill this square with people, kids, dogs, families, and the businesses will come back here!"

"I think a lot of people might stay away, Mayor,"

Gordon said, trying to give Dent a hand. "They're scared."

"They won't be scared when you've got Grissom in that courthouse!" Borg insisted. "I promised that, right?"

Gordon sighed and nodded. The mayor certainly had promised that. He glanced at Dent. The new D.A. shrugged helplessly. They both quickened their pace to catch up with their leader as he climbed the steps of the half-finished reviewing stand.

Knox didn't like the looks of this. The reporters were all gathered around Bob the cartoonist's desk in the corner of the city room. Worse than that, they all smiled when Knox walked in. Knox knew that hungry kind of smile— wolves always hunted in packs.

"Well, well," MacPhee shouted jovially. "Count Dracula! You seen Bigfoot lately?"

"They buried your story on the Batman," Thompson confided with a smirk.

"They bury garbage," MacPhee agreed.

Well, Knox wasn't going to let the human litter of the *Gotham Globe* get him down. Grin firmly in place, he shouted back, "This is the Pulitzer Prize zone, boys. You wait!"

"Oh, Knox?" Bob the cartoonist called sweetly. "I've got something for you!"

He held up a drawing of a human bat, an awful, fanged rodent face sitting on top of a man's body in a business suit. The caption below read: "Have You Seen This Man?"

Well, Thompson, MacPhee, and the others thought this

was the funniest thing that had ever happened in the news office. Knox kept his grin in place. He did wish they could come up with something a little more original.

"Very nice, boys," he replied. "A little more gore on the fangs, perhaps?" He turned and walked on to his office.

Knox stopped outside his door. There was somebody already in there. He could see her through the office window—and *what* he could see.

Well, if he could calm his heart and hormones long enough, they really were only a pair of legs. Only! Any self-respecting panty hose would kill to be seen on legs like that! Knox took another step so that he could look at the rest of her. Not bad at all. With those legs resting on the desk, she was leaning back in Knox's swivel chair, poring over a copy of the *Globe*. Nice figure, nice dress, nice blond hair.

Knox stepped into the office. He couldn't help himself.

"Hel-lo, legs!" he greeted her.

The hat tipped back. A face, fully in keeping with the rest of her form, smiled at him.

"I'm reading your stuff," the face informed him.

"And I'm reading yours," Knox happily agreed. He glanced at an oversized camera bag propped on the corner of his desk. It had a set of monogrammed initials: "V.V."

Legs stood up and offered her hand. Knox took it. She had a firm, no-nonsense handshake.

"Hi," she said. "I'm Vicki Vale."

Knox knew that name from somewhere. He searched his memory.

"Vicki Vale . . . Vicki Vale . . . let's see—" He

snapped his fingers. "*Vogue, Cosmo*—I've seen your stuff." His voice dropped to a more confidential tone. "Listen, you didn't come here to ask me to pose nude—" He paused to wiggle his eyebrows. "—because you're going to need a real long lens."

"Actually," Vicki replied, bright and businesslike, as if he hadn't just made that incredibly tacky remark, "I've been to Corto Maltese."

Corto Maltese? Knox thought. The war zone? That didn't fit at all with the fashion plate he saw before him. She reached into her camera bag and pulled out a small portfolio of photos—combat photos. Knox leafed through them quickly. Guerrillas in hiding, an exploding jeep, government troops torching the peasants' homes, bodies stacked like firewood. It was good stuff. Vicki wasn't afraid to get close to the action. Her photos showed the faces of war and packed a real emotional punch.

"Hey," he said in admiration, "a girl could get hurt doing this stuff." He looked back up at her. "But what are you doing here?"

It was Vicki's turn to raise an eyebrow. "I'm here to see some of the wildlife in Gotham City."

Knox didn't get it. "Wildlife? Like what?"

"Like bats." She pointed down at the papers scattered across Knox's desk. Papers filled with facts, speculation, false starts, even poorly drawn doodles, of Knox's obsession—the human bat.

This couldn't be real. Somebody actually believed him? He looked at Vicki with something akin to wonder.

"Who sent you?"

"No one," she replied with a smile. "I read your piece.

There's something about this that's very interesting to me.''

Interesting? No, Knox thought. This was still too simple.

"What's *your* angle?" he insisted.

"A picture of a guy in a bat suit catching criminals?" She waved a hand in front of her, as if she was writing a headline in the air. " 'Batman Sweeps Crime From Gotham!' My pictures. Your words. This is Pulitzer Prize material.''

Yeah. He'd thought that all along. Hadn't he just said that to the guys in the city room? Knox laughed.

"You're a visionary! Problem is, you're the only one who believes me.'' His elation started to die as reality once again sank in. "I need something tangible. Gordon's got a file on this, but I can't get him on the phone.''

"Gordon?" Vicki gave Knox a conspiratorial wink. "He'll be at Bruce Wayne's benefit, won't he?"

Knox nodded, a bit bewildered. "I don't seem to be on the guest list.'' He stared up toward the ceiling. How was he going to get through to Gordon about this bat? What good was it for Knox to know the truth when he couldn't get anybody to admit it?

What was that? Vicki had stuck something in his field of vision. Something small and white, dangling about three inches from his nose. Something that looked an awful lot like an invitation to Wayne Manor.

Knox almost whooped for joy. He grinned back at Vicki as she put the invitation back in her purse.

"Miss Vale," he asked humbly. "Got a date?"

Miss Vale fluttered her long eyelashes as she shook her head no.

"Will you help me?" she asked.

"Yes," he replied sincerely. "Will you marry me?"

"Perhaps," she answered with a laugh. "Do you snore?"

"I'll learn," he promised with a grin.

Carl Grissom liked the finer things in life. Like this penthouse office. Best view in Gotham City. Or that blond model, Alicia, who looked so good hanging from his arm. That's why he bought the best talent available in Gotham City, from accountants to politicians to enforcers. Men whom he could trust, or whom he disposed of. It had been a long time, though, since he had had to call all of that talent into one room like this.

But that's why he had all this talent on the payroll—from the suit-and-tie boys to the guys who looked as if they'd just walked away from a street fight. He'd brought all the best here—so they could figure out what to do with that new political flea, Harvey Dent.

It had been a long time since Grissom had had to worry about a politician in Gotham City. The mayor was a fool—it was one of the reasons Grissom made sure Borg stayed in office. Commissioner Gordon might have been some trouble, except that Grissom had half of the police lieutenants under Gordon on his payroll. This Dent, though, refused to be bought, and was smart enough to assemble a brand-new team of honest associates. So Grissom had to find a new way to get Dent off his back. He didn't need that kind of headache. That's why he paid these dozen guys sitting around him, to take the headaches for him.

"You've all seen this?" Grissom called out as he waved a copy of the *Globe*. Harvey Dent's picture took up a good part of page one.

Everyone looked up at the sound of their boss's voice —everyone except Jack Napier, practicing his usual one-handed shuffle of a deck of cards.

Grissom looked over at Luce, one of his shirt-and-tie guys with both legal and financial experience. Grissom posed a question:

"Say this son of a bitch makes a connection with us and Axis Chemicals. What kind of damage are we looking at?"

Luce looked uncomfortable as he searched for an answer. "If he ties us in with Axis Chemical, we're dead and buried." He stopped to clear his throat. "We should move immediately."

Jack Napier spoke without looking up from his cards.

"Let's just break in, trash the offices, make off with the books. We can call it 'industrial espionage.' "

Grissom grinned. This was just what he had been expecting. "Smart thinking, Jack. That's the way to go." He paused for a second, as if in thought. "In fact, I'd like you to handle this operation personally."

Jack looked up for the first time. "Me?"

He flipped over a card. Grissom noticed it wasn't a jack for a change. This time, he'd turned up a joker, with the bullet hole right in the middle of its face.

The silence was broken by the chime of Grissom's private elevator. The metal doors slid open, and Alicia stepped out, carrying as many shopping bags as she could handle. As usual, Grissom thought. She was always happy if you let her go shopping. Or at least that's what Grissom had thought till recently.

"Hello, sweetheart," Grissom called, the smile still frozen on his face. "I wonder if you'd mind waiting in the other room."

Alicia nodded from behind her mound of purchases. Her eyes slid over to look at Jack Napier as she disappeared through a door into Grissom's private suite.

Exactly, Grissom thought.

"Thank you, gentlemen," he announced briskly. "That's all for now."

All but one of Grissom's men filed from the room. Jack Napier stood by his chair, his cards still spread on the table before him.

"Carl," Napier asked, "can't you send somebody else? The fumes in that place—"

"Jack," Grissom reiterated, "it's an important job. I need someone I can trust. You're my number-one guy." He smiled and pointed at the table. "Now, don't forget your lucky deck."

Jack nodded and scooped up the cards. Grissom was still smiling as he left the room.

"My friend," he said softly, "your luck is just about to change."

The side door opened. Alicia stepped through to model the first of her many purchases, as she always did.

Grissom would deal with her later. He picked up the phone.

"Get me Lieutenant Eckhardt."

He'd have to give the lieutenant a little extra for his tip—after, of course, Eckhardt made sure Napier was dead.

# C H A P T E R

## Three

Wayne Manor was something else.

Not that Vicki Vale was easily impressed. Her photography had taken her inside castles and palaces, to meet with kings and queens. Wayne Manor wasn't quite in that league—it was merely very large and elegantly appointed. Still, there was something about this place, with its high ceilings and acres of carved mahogany, something that spoke of history and purpose. Wayne Manor might not have been Buckingham Palace, but it was as close as one could get in the States to that feeling of royalty.

Vicki got the feeling that Allie Knox wasn't as used to this kind of surroundings. He tended to slow down as they were shown through the sumptuous hallways on their way to the gallery. And, when they finally reached the room, Allie became frozen in place, unable to do anything but gawk.

Still, after a few minutes, Allie seemed to free himself

up, and began to wander on his own. He still looked a little conspicuous, wandering around in that Sears special polyester-blend suit in a room full of tuxedos. But she couldn't worry about him. He had his job to do, she had hers—and hers was to meet Bruce Wayne. She wanted to find out what drove this so-called philanthropic, millionaire playboy. She had an idea there might be a whole other story there—beyond the human bat.

If she could get to meet Bruce Wayne. She wondered how anybody got introductions around here.

One of the waiters handed a dark-haired fellow in a tuxedo something to sign. So the fellow in the tux must be somebody important. He wasn't bad to look at, either. He signed the paper, and the waiter disappeared.

The fellow in the tux was left holding the pen. He looked around for a place to put it, apparently briefly considering a nearby flowerpot, when the thin, gray-haired, aesthetic fellow—the same one who had admitted Vicki and Allie to the manor—glided to the tuxedo's side to smoothly accept the writing instrument. The gray-haired fellow smiled as his younger counterpart wandered out toward the grand ballroom, and casino night.

Half a dozen roulette wheels and as many blackjack and crap tables had been set up in the huge room, as large as some concert halls Vicki had seen. Small, tasteful, ''Save the Festival!'' banners were hung from the rafters. The floor below was so choked with people that it was difficult to move, with huge mirrors on either side of the great room, reflecting and re-reflecting all the revelry in between, so that it looked as though the party went on forever.

It was quite a sight, with all of Gotham's power elite in all their finery, gambling away their money for charity. Vicki looked at all the jewels sparkling in the light of the great crystal chandeliers and thought of royalty one more time.

She glanced over at Allie Knox, who was once again staring at the ceiling. The aesthetic fellow who had admitted them walked across the room, a tray full of champagne glasses now in his hands. He stopped by Allie and looked up at the ceiling as well.

"Can I help you, sir?"

"You know," Knox replied, "if you cut your bath in half, you'd have my whole apartment."

"We do have a rather large bathroom, sir," the gentleman agreed.

"No," Knox added, "I meant your bath—as in tub."

Allie took a glass of champagne. The gentleman nodded pleasantly and moved on. He walked quickly and assuredly through the crowd. By the time he reached Vicki, half the champagne glasses were gone.

She realized suddenly that he might be the butler—if people still had butlers. That was what butlers did—open doors, serve champagne—wasn't it? A place the size of Wayne Manor almost had to have a butler, didn't it?

The fellow, butler or no, leaned forward to pick up some empty glasses and place them on the tray. He had misjudged the weight of the glasses still taking up half the tray, glasses that now slid and threatened to spill. Vicki stepped to his side and caught the first pair of glasses before they could topple.

The butler righted the other glasses in an instant.

"You okay?" Vicki asked as she replaced the glassware she had saved.

"Yes, thank you," the butler replied with a smile that was both warm and genuine. In all this wealth and power, it was the best smile Vicki had seen all night.

But she hadn't gotten any closer to her goal—meeting Bruce Wayne. The butler had already glided away upon his errands. That good-looking fellow in the tux wandered by again. She turned to him as he passed. It was as good an excuse to talk to him as any.

"Excuse me?" she asked. "Which one of these guys is Bruce Wayne?"

The fellow in the tux looked a little startled. "I—I'm not sure."

Vicki smiled at him anyway. "Thanks."

"Uh—yeah," he replied.

It looked as if Allie was having more luck than she. He had managed to catch Commissioner Gordon over by the crap tables. Vicki excused herself. Now, this could be interesting.

"Commissioner Gordon," Allie began, "Mrs. Gordon. How nice you look tonight." The pleasantries out of the way, he turned to the commissioner.

"Have you heard this crazy rumor that you have opened a file on the Batman? That's not true, is it?"

As an extra special effect, Knox put his fingers behind his head to form two wiggling bat ears. Gordon groaned.

"Knox," he replied, his voice nowhere near as calm as it should be, "for the ninth time, there is no bat. If there were, we would find him. We would arrest him!"

"Find him. Arrest him," Knox agreed. "That's what I always hear. Commissioner, be straight with me—"

Harvey Dent put his hand on Gordon's shoulder. Vicki had been so intent on the exchange between the commissioner and Allie that she hadn't even seen him walk up.

"How's your luck, Jim?"

But before Gordon could answer him, Knox had turned on the fresh prey.

"Mr. Dent. Commissioner Gordon and I were just talking about winged vigilantes. What's your stand?"

Dent looked directly at the reporter. He wouldn't get harried like Gordon. His reply was serious and smooth: "Mr. Knox, we have enough real problems in this city without having to worry about ghosts."

The reply was also meaningless. So Knox's luck was turning bad as well. Vicki was starting to wonder if they'd have anything at all to show for their night in high society.

That's when a policeman came in and waved for Gordon to follow him out of the room. Knox looked over at Vicki. She nodded, and they both walked casually in the direction Gordon had left. The night might still have a few surprises after all.

But where had Gordon gone?

Vicki and Allie walked out the first door, to be confronted by three more, each one closed. One led to a closet, another to a set of stairs leading down. By mutual consensus, they chose the door in the middle, which led to a hallway and another half a dozen doors.

It took them only a couple of minutes to realize they were hopelessly lost. Knox finally chose a door at random, opened it, and charged into the room. Vicki followed. There were no people in here. But there were quite a lot of other things.

"And here we are in the arsenal," Knox quipped. He whistled. "Look at this stuff. Who is this guy?"

It looked as though he had every weapon known to man in this place. Broadswords hung on the wall. Glass cases were filled with everything from blowguns to hand grenades.

The door opened behind them. Allie was too engrossed studying the weapons, but Vicki looked around. It was the good-looking fellow in the tux, champagne glass in his hand. He smiled at her a bit sheepishly. So other people had gotten themselves lost in Wayne Manor too. For some reason, she smiled back.

There was something about this wandering soul, some little-boy-lost quality, perhaps, that Vicki found strangely appealing. She hoped he would stick around. She'd had the feeling, though, from the way he'd reacted the last time they met, that she'd almost scared him away. She'd talk to Allie for a minute, and see if maybe tuxedo would join in.

"Strange," Vicki said to Knox. "He gives to humanitarian causes, and collects all this."

"Probably does it to get goils." Knox's eyebrows wriggled again.

"I think it's his enormous—" Vicki paused thoughtfully. "—bankroll they go for."

Allie laughed ruefully. "Hey, the more they've got, the less they're worth."

Vicki nodded as she took in the size of this room alone "This guy must be the most worthless man in America."

Knox pointed to a long, slightly curved sword in an elaborate silver sheath.

"Where'd this come from?"

"It's Japanese," said a voice behind them.

Vicki and Knox both turned. The good-looking guy in the tux had spoken.

"How do you know?" Knox demanded.

The other guy smiled. "Because I got it in Japan."

But Allie Knox didn't give up that easily.

"Who are you?"

"Oh," the tuxedo said. "Bruce Wayne."

Bruce Wayne? Vicki thought. But he had— But she—

Knox walked quickly across the room, hand extended.

"Allie Knox." They shook hands.

"I've been reading your work," Bruce said. "I like it."

"Great," Knox replied without missing a beat. "Give me a grant."

Bruce grinned, then looked at Vicki. So introductions were finally here. She put out her hand.

"Vicki Vale."

They shook. He had a nice, firm handshake.

"Bruce Wayne."

She looked at him doubtfully. "You sure?"

He replied with that grin again. Vicki realized he could get away with a lot with a smile like that.

"I've seen your photographs of Corto Maltese" was what he did say. "You've got an extraordinary eye."

"Some people think she has two," Allie mentioned as he stepped between them.

Uh-oh, Vicki thought. Male territoriality. Maybe Allie was looking at their date as something more than a convenient reporter's fiction.

"This is an amazing house," she said in an attempt to change the subject. "I'd love to shoot it sometime."

There was a knock at the door. A stiff-backed fellow in a red uniform entered. Vicki's and Knox's eyes met again. How many servants did this Bruce Wayne have?

"Mr. Wayne," began the servant, who must have been some sort of wine steward, "we need to open another five cases of champagne. Will that be all right?"

"Uh—yes, sure," Bruce said with that same, distracted air Vicki had heard when they had first spoken. "Open six."

The steward pivoted smartly and left the room. Bruce Wayne blinked, as if he was trying to remember where he was. He turned back to Vicki.

"Yes. Will you be staying in Gotham for a while?"

"I'd like to," Vicki replied. "I'm intrigued by Allie's giant-bat story."

An overdressed couple paused outside the still-open door to the hall. They waved and called good-night to Mr. Wayne, making polite noises about the wonderful party. Bruce nodded politely back, looking for all the world like he didn't know who they were. His eyes seemed to focus suddenly as he called them both by name. The rich pair waved a final time and departed happily.

Bruce looked back at Vicki.

"Isn't that a little light after a war in Corto Maltese?"

This time, it took Vicki a second to remember their conversation. Oh, yes. The bat story.

"Light?" she replied with a small, sarcastic edge. "And what do you do for a living?"

There was a discreet cough at the doorway. Vicki looked up to see the butler.

"Sir?" the butler mentioned. "Commissioner Gordon was compelled to leave."

"Thank you, Alfred," Bruce said without looking.

"Ahem," Alfred added somewhat more forcefully. "Sir. *Very* unexpectedly."

"Oh," Bruce replied, looking at the butler at last. "Thank you, Alfred." That slightly sheepish look was back on his face as he turned to Vicki. "I hope you'll excuse me."

He looked right into her eyes. She looked right back into his. They both knew this wasn't the end of something.

"Sure," she said.

He looked away. Vicki blinked. It was like some sort of line that held them together had suddenly snapped and she was once again free to look other places in the room.

Bruce put his glass down on the edge of a table and started from the room.

"Sir," Alfred interrupted, "I think perhaps this way."

Bruce looked at his butler more alertly. "Oh, yes . . . thanks. Oh, Alfred, they need some more wine in the front and someone named Mrs. Daly wanted a copy of the menu." He started to walk across the room to the far door. "Oh, and Alfred, give Mr. Knox a grant."

He winked at Knox as he turned and walked rapidly from the room. Alfred picked up Mr. Wayne's glass and effortlessly caught up with his employer in the far doorway. The butler shut the door behind them.

Knox stared at the closed door. "Nice talkin' to you, Bruce." He glanced at Vicki. "Now, are the rich odd? Yes, they are." He waited for a moment, then added: "Hello? Vicki?"

She realized she was still half looking at the door where Bruce Wayne had disappeared. "Sorry, I was . . ." She tried to gather her thoughts. "He's comp-lic-ated." She said at last, slowing the syllables as if the new emphasis would explain it all.

"I said odd," Knox insisted. Vicki realized there might be a little jealousy there.

"Mmm," was her answer.

"Ah," Knox replied, totally dissatisfied. "Well, you're not the only fan around here. This guy loves himself. There are mirrors in every room."

Vicki realized Knox was right. There had been huge mirrors on two walls of the grand ballroom. And here were the two of them, standing before another mirror, eight feet wide, that ran from floor to ceiling.

"Bruce Wayne," Allie added sarcastically. "Maybe it should be Bruce *Vain*."

If you only knew, Mr. Knox. Bruce Wayne took a final moment to watch Vicki and the reporter in the video monitor. The state-of-the-art surveillance camera had silently recorded everything in the armory from behind the one-way glass of the full-length mirror. Of course, it was only one of three dozen monitors, designed to record everything that happened in and around Wayne Manor. And it was one of those other monitors that demanded his attention.

Guests moved backward with exaggerated speed as Wayne rewound the tape. Ah. He punched a button on the console before him. This is what he wanted.

A patrolman talked to Commissioner Gordon on the screen.

"—anonymous tip," the patrolman was saying. "Napier's cleaning out Axis Chemical."

"Good Lord," Gordon replied, excited and agitated at the same time. "If we could put our hands on him, we'd have Grissom! Why wasn't I told about this? Who's in charge of the—"

"Eckhardt, sir."

Gordon blanched. "Oh, my God—" He reached over and grabbed his coat.

The screen went blank.

Bruce Wayne smiled. This was just what he needed. He stood and walked back out into the cave.

It was time.

# C H A P T E R

## Four

Jack didn't like this one bit. He hadn't had to handle this kind of a job in years. Breaking and entering, petty theft —you paid guys to do those things for you, and you expected those guys to take the fall if they got caught.

But Jack still worked for Grissom. For now, he had to do what the Boss told him. He wasn't ready to make his move in that department—yet.

There was something about this job that made him want to move that much sooner.

The break-in had gone fine so far. His boys had driven up in their unmarked vans and taken out the guards without any trouble at all. They had dismantled the burglar alarms in a matter of seconds, the safe was exactly where Grissom had said it should be, and the guy with the blowtorch would have it open in a minute or less. So why was Jack so uneasy?

Part of that was simple to answer. Even though he had

always had a way with chemistry, Jack had never liked fumes. But now, even with his silk handkerchief over his nose and mouth, he could still feel the noxious gases in this place seeping into his lungs. But there was something else wrong here, something that didn't quite fit. Jack had had that funny feeling ever since he had been in Grissom's office and turned over a joker instead of a jack.

The safecracker flicked off his torch. He reached out with an asbestos glove and opened the door.

"Empty," he announced.

Shit! Jack thought. He had known it.

That's when the alarms went off.

"We've been ratted out here, boys!" Jack yelled to his cronies. "Let's get out of this mess!"

He led the way out of the office, an office two stories above the refinery floor. This whole deal got worse the more he thought about it. They were sitting ducks up here. And Jack had the feeling there'd be enough guns waiting down below for a shooting gallery.

"Freeze!" someone yelled from the floor of the refinery. Jack glanced down. It was a cop, of course. One of a dozen or so cops Jack could see. Just like there were bound to be more cops outside the building and around the vans. Cops who had to have been here even before the alarms went off, cops who had been fed some very special information from very high in the Grissom organization. Jack knew that some of these cops probably had very special instructions, too. He knew all too well how Grissom operated. After all, how many times had Jack personally carried out the Boss's instructions?

If he didn't get out of here fast, Jack Napier was a dead

man. He had gotten himself caught in a classic setup. When Grissom wanted to get rid of you, he made sure it was done right.

A couple of Jack's gunmen shot down at the cops. The cops jumped for cover, but a second later they opened up as well, bullets from a dozen guns spraying among the ceiling pipes.

Half the guys ducked back into the office. But that was suicide—there was no other way out from there. The only escape was across the catwalks. Jack yelled for the others to follow him. Then he ran.

Bullets flew past him, embedding themselves in the pipes cluttered all around. Fluids burst forth from dozens of new holes; liquids in every unnatural shade of green and red and purple and brown rained down across the catwalks. Who knew what that stuff was, or what it could do to you? Jack ran through the poisonous downpour, careful not to slip on the wet metal underneath his feet. He would just have to hope that he could wash the chemicals off before they did any permanent damage—

There was a great clang as a bullet ricocheted off a metal railing inches from his hand.

—that is, Jack reflected, if something else didn't damage him first.

He'd get to the bottom of this, even if he had to shoot Eckhardt personally.

Commissioner Gordon nodded to one of his men. He'd brought fifty along, all handpicked, to make sure this job was done right. His lieutenant punched the button.

Luck was with them. The electricity was still working.

The huge, corrugated steel door rose with a metallic groan to show the loading dock of the Axis Chemical Company.

There were policemen on the other side of the door, officers who looked around in confusion at the new opening. Eckhardt was in the middle of the cops. The commissioner wondered what kind of excuse the lieutenant would have this time.

"What the *hell* is going on here?" Gordon roared.

The commissioner marched forward. He wanted the men to recognize him, to stop any accidental gunfire. Eckhardt might be crooked, but most, if not all, of the other men were just regular cops trying to do their job.

Eckhardt had gone too far this time. Not that they wouldn't have gotten him—eventually. There had been an internal investigation going on concerning certain officers on the force suspected of taking money from Boss Grissom. Eckhardt had been on the top of that list. They had been days away from pinning the charges on him. Now, Gordon thought, they might be able to make those charges stick in a matter of minutes.

Gordon walked quickly through the crowd. Eckhardt stared at him, trying to look angry. But, underneath that anger, Gordon could see the fear.

The commissioner wished he knew exactly what Eckhardt was up to. According to their informer, Napier was being set up. For some reason, Grissom must want Napier put out of the way, and was using Eckhardt and the Gotham City Police Force to do it. Whatever that reason was, it made Napier all that much more valuable to Gordon and the D.A.'s case against Grissom and his associates.

Lieutenant Eckhardt yelled as the commissioner approached. "Christ, what are you trying to do? Blow the collar?"

But Gordon had had enough of Eckhardt.

"I'm in charge here. Not Carl Grissom."

The anger evaporated from Eckhardt's face. He looked like a frightened rabbit facing a wolf.

Gordon raised his voice as he turned to the other policemen.

"I want Jack Napier taken alive. I repeat—any man who opens fire on Jack Napier will answer to *me*!"

He looked around. Eckhardt was gone.

If that's the way you want to play it, Lieutenant, Gordon thought. One way or another, Eckhardt was going to pay for this. Dent and Borg were going to get their new Gotham City, one way or another.

The commissioner drew his gun and walked into the plant.


Jack be nimble. Jack be quick.

Napier almost laughed as the nursery rhyme rattled through his head. He ran down a final set of metal stairs and landed, still alive, on the cement floor of the Axis Chemical Company.

He had always liked little rhymes and sayings. That's why he had those special words he always liked to use when he killed people.

*You ever danced—*

Somebody yelled from across the room. They had spotted him again.

You're not out of this one yet, Jack boy.

Napier looked around. Time for a little diversion. He

had to run a little bit farther before he could jump over that candlestick.

*—danced with the devil—*

There were a lot of diversions in a chemical factory. Some of them quite deadly. Jack threw a switch here, twisted a dial there, running all the time. The huge machines exploded with sound. Jack couldn't hear his running feet anymore. He couldn't even hear the bullets following him. Everything was drowned beneath the automated thunder.

*—devil by the pale—*

Jack turned a corner and hesitated only long enough to throw another switch or two. Or three. The floor was shaking with the noise now. It felt like the whole place was going to fall apart. Jack realized they probably never had all these machines operating at the same time—until now. Giant vats of chemicals spun overhead, spilling their contents into even larger basins on either side of him.

*—the pale moonlight?*

Machines roaring, acids bubbling, people screaming, bullets flying—it all made a very special sort of chaos. Jack decided he liked chaos. It certainly made it easier for him to get away. And, once he was free, he had a little business to attend to.

Grissom gets the police. The police try to get Jack. But Jack gets Grissom instead. Napier grinned at how tidy a package it made. It was all a little game.

*You ever danced with the devil by the pale moonlight?*

Machines and bullets and screams and fumes. He wasn't free yet. And if he didn't get free, he could never get even. And that wouldn't be fair at all.

In that case, Jack decided, it was more than a game. Now it was all one big, never-ending joke.

Gordon thought he was walking into hell. The gunfire echoed back and forth through the cavernous room, punctuating half-heard human cries, some of anger, some of pain. The air smelled of smoke and acid. The place was huge, and lit by floodlights some fifty feet above the floor. It wasn't the best way to light a place this size. The spots bounced all too brightly from the pipes and machines high above the ground, but down here on the floor they did little more than produce a confusion of shadows. Axis Chemical probably thought they were giving enough illumination for their night watchmen. They probably never suspected they'd have to fight a war.

Someone screamed on a catwalk far overhead. Gordon saw the figure slump back against the railing, a gun falling with a clang from unresisting fingers. There were others up on the catwalks. Gordon could see two others silhouetted in the spots, running from their dead companion. He couldn't see who was firing from the floor. He assumed it had to be some of his men.

Gordon caught the hint of movement farther overhead, the glimmer of light against metal, a flash of yellow in the dark. There was an audible clang as a pair of boots hit the metal catwalk. Someone else was up there now, lost in the shadows between the lights.

The two gunmen must have seen the newcomer more clearly than Gordon could. They didn't consider him a friend. One of the hoods ran back the other way. The other pointed his gun at the newcomer.

But the newcomer was moving too, lifting a weapon, shooting—but not a bullet. Gordon could have sworn it was some kind of short spear, as it hooked into the gunman's jacket, spinning him around. The hood lost his balance. He dropped his gun as he grabbed for the railing. But he was slipping too fast. He screamed as he fell from the catwalk—

—and stopped, thirty feet in the air, the hook in his jacket attached to a rope, a rope that went back up to the catwalk, and a man who had stepped out into the light.

"Oh, my God," Gordon whispered. He could see the new figure clearly now.

It was a man dressed as a bat.

Jack felt as if he had been running forever. There had to be some way out of here. He headed for the far end of the factory floor, hoping to find some kind of emergency exit.

A motor started up in front of him, from a switch he hadn't thrown. A huge, steel door started to rise not twenty feet away. Jack stopped. Maybe this was his ticket out of here.

He gave up that idea before the door had reached his waist. It was the twenty pairs of legs he saw on the other side that dissuaded him—twenty pairs all dressed in police blue. He heard gunfire on the floor behind him. Where could he go now? He heard the police shouting to each other on the other side of the door.

Jack decided to take the stairs. If he couldn't find a door, maybe he could find a window. But those cops behind him were awfully close.

Then Jack spotted the fire ax. Maybe it was time for another diversion. There was that skull and crossbones by the stairs, the one on that rusted steel tank that bore the words DANGER! HIGHLY TOXIC!

Yes, Jack thought. This would do quite nicely. He swung the ax with every ounce of adrenaline-pumped strength in him. The blade cut neatly into the tank's largest patch of rust, and when he yanked the ax free, toxic waste burst forth to flood the floor.

The cops fled, running into each other in their haste to escape. Mission accomplished. Jack threw his weapon to the ground, staring with fascination for a moment at the bubbles that formed as the viscous fluids ate away the ax handle. He climbed the stairs, hidden from the shooting by two more of the great metal tanks.

There was another sound here, besides the guns and machines, a great, whooshing sound—the noise of rushing water. Jack realized he must be near the sluice gates, the place where Axis Chemical dumped those fine by-products that made Gotham's East River what it was today. He looked toward the noise and saw an open window.

The stairs and this end of the catwalk were in shadow. But to reach that window, he'd have to pass beneath two spotlights, a real moving target. Jack couldn't see any other way. If this was all a joke, it was time to get to the punchline. He ran.

And he was at the window. Not a single shot was fired. All of Jack's diversions must have worked. He had only to climb the railing, and then—

Somebody grabbed him. Black-clad arms snaked around

Jack's rib cage, reaching for his neck. The jerk was trying to get him in some sort of goddamned wrestling hold.

"Jesus!" Jack yelled as he tried to break free. Who was this guy?

"Hold it!" yelled a voice down on the floor.

What now? Jack despaired. He had almost gotten out of here. Then he looked down and saw the speaker was his old friend Bob, with a gun pointed neatly at the police commissioner. Good old Bob.

"Let him go, or I'll do Gordon," Bob announced. Good old Bob had always had a way with words.

Jack saw Eckhardt down below. Of course! Who else could Grissom get to do this dirty work? Well, once Jack got out of this, he and the fat boy had a little business.

Jack felt the wrestling hold disappear. He stood again and straightened his coat, then ran a hand through his hair. He glanced around at his attacker.

Now, this was crazy.

The guy was maybe six feet tall, well muscled and wearing some kind of *bat* costume. Maybe, Jack thought, he really was some kind of professional wrestler. The bat had backed off a bit, giving them both some breathing space, but his eyes were fixed on Jack.

Jack grinned at him.

"Nice outfit," he remarked.

There was no reply. Well, what did Jack expect from a guy in a bat suit?

"Jack?" Bob called up. "Let's get out of here."

Jack saw the .38 lying on the catwalk. That was the problem with a messy setup like this—people were dropping guns all over the place. And that's when he saw Eckhardt turn to leave.

Jack grabbed the gun.

"Eckhardt!" he yelled. "Think about the future!"

Jack fired once. Eckhardt sprawled on the floor, dead. Jack was always good at this sort of thing. He turned the gun on Gordon.

But then the nut in the bat suit moved. Jack glanced over. There seemed to be a question on the bat guy's face—a question or a challenge. Jack smiled. Nice outfit or no, you didn't cross Jack Napier.

He fired, point blank, at the bat.

But the bat wasn't still. He did something with his cape, swinging it forward.

The bullet ricocheted, bounced right off the goddamned costume, straight back to Jack.

He felt the pain in his cheek. Jack's hand was there before he knew what he was doing. His fingers were covered with blood. He had been shot in the face.

He fell backward, off the catwalk, over the railing. No! His hand grabbed the catwalk's edge.

He looked down. Below him, on the factory floor, was a bubbling vat twenty feet across. He had to pull himself up. But he had no strength. The whooshing sound was much louder here. He must be close to the sluice gates. His face was burning off.

His fingers slipped from the walkway, but he grabbed a pipe just below instead. A round, slippery pipe. The guy in the bat suit reached down from where he knelt on the catwalk, and grabbed Jack's wrist.

Jack lost the pipe, but the Batman held him. His grip wasn't firm; Jack could feel the bat's cloth-covered fingers slipping away. He tried to reach his own hand up to grip the other's wrist, but there was no strength left. Even through his burning nostrils, he could smell the fumes below. There was nothing left. Was this the end of the joke?

He felt his wrist slide again, felt the bat's grasp slip by his fingers.

Jack fell.

He screamed all the way down.


The scream echoed around them as Napier plunged into the bubbling slime.

Gordon shuddered. Nobody, not even Jack Napier, should die like that.

"Goddammit!" he yelled. "We had him!"

But his men weren't quite so emotional. With Napier gone, they had trained their guns on the Batman. A pair of police officers had worked their way to either end of the catwalk. They had him trapped.

Well, Gordon thought, they'd have something to show for their night's work.

"Hold it right there," he ordered.

The Batman raised his hands. The officers approached him from either side.

The bat flicked something at a nearby wall.

The room exploded with light, like an indoor fireworks display. Gordon shielded his eyes. The cops up there had been blinded. Where the Batman stood a moment ago, there was a pillar of white smoke.

"Look!" somebody yelled as a hook and line emerged from the smoke to latch on to a window overhead. Some of the men had started to fire, but the Batman was already shooting upward along the line, lost in the shadows above the lights.

The police stopped shooting into the dark. The bat was gone.

"Who *is* this guy?" somebody asked.

"I don't know," Gordon replied, "and until we find out, put a lid on it."

His men finally seemed to be getting things under control. One by one, the remaining gunmen were giving up. But he had seen the Batman! This night had given Gordon a lot more questions than answers, and, with Eckhardt and Napier dead, there were probably some things he'd never find out.

There was only one thing Gordon was certain of: He'd see the Batman again.

First, it had been only his face.

Now everything was burning. He forced himself to think. Where was he? What could he do?

Jack had fallen into the vat, but he hadn't stayed there. He had been pushed, with tremendous force, out with a wall of water, hanging for an instant in the open air. He had gone out the sluice gate, and fallen, forty feet, into the East River. The river that still threatened to drown him—if he didn't burn up first.

There was something in his hand, something small and hard, with corners. Jack opened his eyes in the moonlight. Even with the water in his face, even through the pain, he could see, somehow, that he had grabbed his lucky deck.

The ace of spades slipped away in the current, the bullet hole clear through the black center. Than another ace, a nine, a deuce, and all four jacks, card after card carried away by the torrent. He gasped for breath as he felt the last of his lucky deck slip from his hand.

The last card was a joker.

# C H A P T E R

## Five

BATMAN FOILS ROBBERY!
JACK NAPIER DEAD!
WHO IS MASKED VIGILANTE?

Alexander Knox had never seen anything sweeter than those headlines. Gordon would have to tell him the truth now.

"Yes, Commissioner," Knox said into the phone. "If there's no Batman, then who dropped this guy Napier into the acid?" He grabbed the portable microphone with his free hand. "Wait a minute, I want to get this on tape."

There was a loud click, then a dial tone. Gordon had hung up on him. Knox grinned. You can run, Commissioner, but you cannot hide from this ace investigative reporter. Sooner or later, you'll have to answer for everything.

He looked up. Vicki had come into the room while he was on the phone. She was hanging up a series of photos on his bulletin board—it looked like some kind of a map. Bob the cartoonist peeked in the door, grinned at Knox, and tacked up a present of his own: a drawing of the Batman, with his arm on a somewhat startled Knox's shoulder. Jokers, Knox thought. There're always jokers.

He hung up the phone.

"Vicki Vale!" he called, pointing to himself. "Let me introduce you to Nostradamus!"

Vicki smiled and shook her head. "Look at this, Allie."

Knox stood up and walked over to get a better look at the bulletin board. Vicki had put together a sort of montage map using aerial photographs.

She pointed rapidly to small yellow pins she'd placed in the photos. "Here's the inner city, and here's Axis Chemicals. Here are the sightings so far."

Knox shook his head in wonder. "Did you do this? This is great."

Vicki shrugged her lovely shoulders self-deprecatingly.

"Maybe the Batman's got some sort of flight pattern or something."

"Yeah!" Knox answered with growing enthusiasm. "Tonight we'll walk the trail."

This time Vicki's smile was a little apologetic. "Tomorrow, maybe. I've got a date with Bruce Wayne. Sorry."

Knox couldn't stand it.

"Bruce Wayne?" he demanded. Maybe his voice was a little louder than it should have been. "No, a date is when two people go out to enjoy each other. A date with Bruce Wayne is when he goes out to a restaurant with mirrors, by *himself*!"

He looked back at Vicki. Her face was awfully close to his. Knox suddenly forgot all about shouting. God, look at those big blue eyes, those perfect lips. She was closer still. He closed his eyes.

She kissed him on the forehead.

His eyes opened. She was still smiling.

"You're awfully sweet to be concerned," she said brightly, "but thanks anyway."

With that, she left.

Bruce Wayne? Knox thought. What could she see in Bruce Wayne? What did he have that Allie Knox didn't, except maybe money and a fabulous mansion and money and blueblood breeding and money and social connections and even more money? And now he was going to get the girl, too? That wasn't fair!

Well, ace investigative reporters knew what to do when things weren't fair. Certain private lives were about to get a public viewing. He picked up the phone.

"Copy, get me the morgue."

"Morgue here," a bored voice answered.

"Morgue," Knox replied, excited enough now for both of them. "Give me all you got on Bruce Wayne."

Vicki had been a lot of places around the world, but, somehow, none of them had been as nice as this—the two of them horseback riding in the fields behind Wayne Manor, the late-summer air cut by the first breezes of autumn, the setting sun turning the entire world to red and gold. She was sorry when they caught sight of the stables again. There were some moments, she thought, that should never end.

Bruce reined in his mount, a dark stallion with just a hint of white, as they reached the stable yard. Vicki quickly followed on the polite but frisky strawberry roan she had been given. She looked over at Bruce as they both dismounted.

"You're not bad on a horse."

He raised an eyebrow in disbelief as he groomed his horse with a curry comb. "Horses love me. I keep falling off. Maybe that's why they love me. You should see me. I'm one big mass of bruises."

Vicki couldn't help but laugh. "Maybe we can arrange a little examination?"

Bruce put the curry comb on a rail and turned to her.

"Yeah, how about right now?" he asked quickly.

Vicki almost felt as though she should take a step away.

"Just kidding," he admitted.

He flashed his quick, mischievous grin. "You thought you had me, didn't you?" He started to walk up toward the main house, then stopped so that she could walk beside him.

Vicki looked over at her date, even more dashing in the reddish glow of the setting sun. There is something about you, Bruce Wayne. Something that tries to be very hard, almost impenetrable, but is really very, very vulnerable. Vicki thought about how quickly he'd picked up on her innuendo. She'd had that sort of problem with men before. But with Bruce, the "how about right now" wasn't the blundering sexual come-on she might get from an Allie Knox. With Bruce, the comment seemed more of a defense mechanism, as if he had something to hide.

They walked the rest of the way to the manor in silence.

Bruce led her to a broad patio at the rear of the house and asked her to sit in a chair at one side of a white table. Alfred appeared silently, bearing a bottle of champagne. He smiled briefly at Vicki. She smiled back. Then the butler was gone.

It took Bruce a long moment to get the champagne uncorked. He obviously gave this work to other hands most of the time. The cork popped at last, and Bruce managed to get most of the champagne into a couple of handy glasses.

There was a discreet cough from the patio door.

"The Historical Society called to remind you of the banquet," Alfred announced. "Should I say you'll be there?"

"Yes, absolutely," Bruce agreed a bit distractedly. He glanced at Vicki. "I'll be there."

The butler turned to leave.

"Alfred—" Bruce interrupted his retreat. "Which society?"

"Historical," Alfred replied.

"Oh, yeah, right," Bruce replied brightly, as if a veil had been lifted from his eyes. "Yes."

Alfred smiled politely and disappeared into the house.

Vicki looked over at Bruce. "That Alfred's great."

"I can't find my socks without him," Bruce agreed. "Been with the family since I was born."

He yawned as he finished pouring the champagne.

"Am I keeping you up?" Vicki asked with a grin.

He looked a little sheepish. "I'm sorry. I've got a lot going on at the moment."

"Like who?" she needled.

That seemed to fluster him even more. "No, just business. I'll be honest with you, I bore myself silly." He lifted his glass in her direction, as if in a toast. "Tell me about you."

Vicki considered as she cradled her champagne glass in her open palms. What was there to tell?

"I take pictures," she began. "And I love doing it. I feel naked without a camera."

One corner of Bruce's mouth turned up slightly. "Well, we'd better get you one." She found herself smiling in return.

"Go on," he urged.

"I've been floating around for a while, doing fashion," she continued. "It was all right . . . I don't know. Things change." There was something about this man, maybe his intensity, that made her really want to explain the way she felt, in a way that perhaps she hadn't even explained it to herself.

"How old are you?" she asked him at last.

"Just turned thirty-five," he answered.

About what she'd guessed. "You've probably had it happen too. You wake up one morning and say, 'Hey! This is who I am!' " She paused to take a sip of her champagne. "I see things through cameras. All kinds of things. Not just long legs and great skirts but . . . things. You know?"

"I'm not sure," he replied.

"Well." She put down her glass with a shrug. "I just picked up and left."

"What did you see?" he prompted.

Vicki sighed. "A lot of hotels. A little terror. A little love once in a blue moon."

"A little terror," Bruce repeated slowly, considering every word. "A little love."

"It's out there," she replied softly. "I was never in the right place at the right time, I guess."

Bruce had no answer for that. He stared out at his estate and the last rays of the fading sun.

So far, Vicki realized, they had been talking only about her.

"You're a little elusive, Mr. Wayne," she ventured. "I feel there's a lot going on in there."

He glanced back at her. "Oh—not really."

"Come on," she demanded quietly. "Say what you're thinking."

It took him a moment to start.

"I was just thinking how beautiful you looked on that horse . . . and that—it's kind of nice to have someone here who notices things."

Such a simple thing to say, Vicki thought. Somehow, it made her feel very warm inside.

"See," she said with a smile. "I do have an extraordinary eye." She reached her hand across the table.

"Two," he replied. He took her hand in his. They both looked out at a sunset that might go on forever.

She'd had a little too much champagne. The only way she could keep from falling was to hang on to Bruce's arm. How were women supposed to drink and walk in high heels, anyway?

He led her into the entryway to Wayne Manor, a modest room about the same size as the combined editorial offices of the *Gotham Globe*. It was all so opulent, and so unreal.

She waved at the staircases to either side.

"I feel like I'm in Paris in the thirties." She giggled. "Is this fair? I'm half drunk and you're not even—"

She almost lost her balance again, but Bruce caught her in time. He'd probably get her a car now and send her home. He was such a gentleman. That was Vicki's problem. She was always getting stuck with gentlemen.

"Two drinks and I'm flying," he admitted. She looked up at him, safe in his arms.

"Why are you afraid of flying?" she whispered.

They kissed at last.

# C H A P T E R

## Six

Jack couldn't see much with the bandages. And he didn't feel like doing too much looking around this pigsty, either. He'd done enough gazing out broken windows, read too much subliterate graffiti. He'd be glad to get out of here. This kind of hole was too low-rent even for rats.

Dr. Davis busied himself with his outdated instruments. The doctor always busied himself with something. It was so much easier than having to talk to the patients. Still, Davis had gotten a couple of bullets out of Jack before, and both patient and doctor had survived. A quack like Davis was the best you could do when you were hiding out.

The doctor turned to him at last, a nervous twitch fighting with his insincere smile.

"Well, let's see how we did."

Slowly, much too slowly, he snipped the bandages away, then pulled free the last of the gauze.

Davis took a step away. He gasped, the smile gone, his eyes wide with something like fright.

Jack didn't like that expression.

"Mirror," he ordered.

The doctor only stood there, openmouthed.

"Mirror!" Jack demanded.

The doctor cleared his throat, quickly picking up a hand mirror from the table at his side. He passed the mirror to Jack. Davis's hand was shaking so hard that it took Jack a minute to grab the handle. He pulled the mirror in front of his face.

Oh, God!

The mirror slipped from his hands to shatter on the floor. Jack heard a low sob, which he realized must have come from his own throat.

"You—you understand that the nerves were completely severed, Mr. Napier," Davis explained hastily.

Jack began to laugh.

The doctor pushed at the table behind him, rattling the outdated surgical equipment.

"You see what I had to work with here—"

Jack laughed even louder. The doctor covered his face, afraid to look at him.

"I'm sure," Davis muttered, "with the proper recon—recon—reconstructive surgery—"

Jack couldn't take it anymore. He walked out of Davis's office, slamming the door behind him. And he laughed and laughed, screams of laughter echoing up and down the tenement halls.

He had been wrong. The joke wasn't over yet.

It was just beginning.

* * *

God, what a day. He was getting too old for this.

He had thought the hot shower would help, but he was just too weary from all the phone calls, the legwork, the deals and arguments. That was the problem when you lost your number-two man. He had had to reshuffle the whole organization.

Grissom turned off the water and grabbed a towel. Too bad about Jack, but he knew as well as anybody what happened when you stepped out of line. Carl Grissom hadn't gotten where he was today by being a nice guy.

He heard the elevator door open in the next room and someone settle with a sigh into one of the overstuffed chairs. It was Alicia, back from her daily shopping spree. Security would have called him if it was anyone else.

"That you, sugar bumps?" Grissom called.

She didn't answer. Probably too busy looking over what she bought today. He wrapped the big towel around his waist and grabbed a smaller one to dry his hair as he walked into the other room.

Alicia wasn't in her usual chair. Grissom looked around the room. He could just make the silhouette. There was someone sitting behind his desk, someone totally covered by a raincoat, scarf, and oversized top hat. It didn't look like Alicia.

"Who the hell are you?"

"It's me," the muffled figure answered dryly. "Sugar bumps."

Grissom recognized that voice. "Jack?"

Maybe the other man nodded. It was too hard for Grissom to tell with all that clothing. They said he'd been shot, that he'd fallen into a vat of acid. How could he have survived? And what did he want now?

Grissom decided it was time to start covering his tracks.

"Thank God you're alive," he said with all the sincerity he could muster. "I heard you'd been—"

"Fried," Jack interrupted caustically. "Is that what you heard?"

Jack stood up. Grissom tried to think what he could say next, to keep things under control. Grissom always kept things under control. But there was a slight problem with that control just now—Jack would have a gun.

"You set me up!" Jack spat out the words. "Over a girl. You must be insane."

No, Jack, Grissom thought. I'm not the crazy one around here. He could feel his heart beating, much too fast. This kind of excitement wasn't good for someone Grissom's age. He edged casually around the corner of his desk. If he could only reach his desk drawer . . .

"Don't bother," Jack remarked.

Grissom stopped and looked at the gun pointing at his belly. This time, Jack was serious.

"Your life won't be worth spit," Grissom announced.

"I been dead once already," Jack replied matter-of-factly. "It's very liberating. You have to think of it as therapy."

Jack raised the gun so that it pointed at Grissom's heart. Grissom couldn't let this happen. Jack had to listen to reason. Grissom had gotten out of worse than this.

"Jack—listen. We'll cut a deal."

The gun didn't move. "Jack? Jack's dead, my friend. You can call me Joker."

Then this "Joker" took off his hat and coat. Grissom wished he had left them on. He hardly looked like Jack Napier at all anymore. His flesh was bone white, his hair as green as artificial turf. But it was his mouth that was really horrible. Something that happened in the accident must have frozen his flesh that way, his lips much too red against the rest of his skin, his mouth warped into a never-ending rictus grin.

"As you can see," Jack replied, "I'm much happier."

He giggled. He really was crazy. But his gun had moved when he took off his disguise. The muzzle was pointed at the floor. This, Grissom knew, was his only chance.

The giggling turned to laughter as Grissom lunged for the desk drawer. He laughed even harder as he turned his gun on Grissom and fired. And fired. And fired.

Bruce Wayne couldn't sleep.

He'd gotten himself involved at the worst possible time.

He looked over at the woman who slept beside him in the king-size bed. She was a remarkable woman: witty, intelligent, and very beautiful. Her hair cascaded across the pillow. It seemed to glow in the moonlight. Her eyes closed, mouth open ever so slightly in sleep, she looked very peaceful, even innocent. Sleep brings out the child in all of us, he thought. She looked like a painting by one of the Pre-Raphaelites, even more beautiful in the moonlight than she had been in the glow of the setting sun.

Why did she have to come into his life now? After all his hard work, all his resolve, all his denial?

Maybe, Bruce thought, that was the answer. Maybe this regimen, this goal, this quest he had given himself was simply too much for any one man. Everyone had their needs, after all. As much as you tried to avoid them, they'd come back, one way or another.

And his needs had been answered by Vicki Vale.

The grandfather clock in the hall struck four. He looked at his watch. His watch said four as well. He climbed quietly out of bed.

She was so beautiful.

There were things he had to do.

He stepped to the window and looked out at the moon.


*You ever danced with the devil by the pale moonlight?*
Too bad he didn't have the chance to say those words to Grissom. He had used up all his bullets instead. Ah, well. His life as the Joker had just begun.

The Joker sat in the dark. That way, he didn't have to look at Grissom's body, crumpled in a corner. He'd have to get someone to take it away, someone he could trust. That was the problem with being a criminal mastermind. All these niggling little details.

Still, this was a nice office that Grissom had given him—the Boss had taste in some things. And what a great view it had, with the city beneath him—a thousand sparkling lights, stretching to the limits of the window. And overhead, the moon, almost full again, his own, personal night-light.

The Joker sighed in contentment.

"Gotham City. It always brings a smile to my face."

He glanced at the desk and saw the headline on the *Gotham Globe*, large enough to be legible in the moonlight:

WINGED FREAK TERRORIZES GOTHAM'S GANG-LAND!

Nice of Grissom to leave him this newspaper—a little blood-splattered, perhaps, but otherwise quite readable. He picked up the paper and hummed a happy tune.

"Watch it, Batman." He chuckled merrily. "Wait until they get a load of me."

Was that man going to sleep forever? And why **had** he gotten out of bed to sleep on a sofa?

Vicki was almost dressed, and all that Bruce had done was to roll over and mumble something incoherent.

He rolled again as she walked past. One eye struggled to open.

"Bruce," Vicki said softly. "I'm late, but I've a proposition."

He blinked and sat up. Actually, Vicki thought, he woke up pretty fast.

"I'll make us lunch tomorrow," she explained. "I'll show you some of my photos." She pulled a brush from her purse and ran it through her hair. "Will you come?"

Bruce stretched and smiled at her for a second before his expression became more doubtful.

"Sure. Oh, no—I—I can't make it."

She stopped brushing and looked back at Bruce.

"Oh. Is anything wrong?"

He shook his head sharply, as if to rid it of cobwebs.

"No—I—I've got a real important meeting."

She put her brush away. "Well . . . later in the day?"

"No—I—I've got to leave town for a few days."

Vicki frowned. Each time he answered her, it seemed less certain than the answer before. "Well, when you get back," she said at last. She closed her purse and managed a smile. This was only a one-night thing, after all.

"Hey," she said more brightly than before. "I've got to get moving. See you."

She kissed him lightly on the cheek and walked away.

"Yeah," Bruce replied quietly. "I'll see you."

And then she was out of the room.

Alfred met her at the end of the hall. He opened the front door for her.

"So nice to see you again, Miss Vale."

"Yeah." Vicki smiled at the gentleman's gentleman. "I guess I'll see you when you guys get back."

"Back, ma'am?" Alfred asked with the politest of frowns. "We're here for quite a while, I believe."

"Oh," Vicki replied, her cheer suddenly deflated. "Never mind. See you."

She stepped through the doorway and walked away from her one night in Wayne Manor. So much for dreams where millionaire playboys were concerned.

This was the first time he'd been in Alicia's apartment in ever so long. The place hadn't improved in the meantime. But the Joker had an idea for a change or two.

She'd come in already, but she hadn't noticed him. She was far too busy in the other room with her dress bags and packages. There! He could see her in the doorway.

"Honey!" he called.

She turned around. She dropped her packages. She screamed.

Was that any way to greet your lover? And here he was, in smoking jacket and slippers, dry martini at his side, reading the evening paper while waiting for his Alicia to come home.

Oh, well. Perhaps a little conversation would break the ice.

"You wouldn't *believe*," the Joker quipped, "what happened to me today."

Alicia fell to the floor in a dead faint.

Then again, the Joker considered, perhaps their relationship needed some work.

This is the way it was supposed to be! All of Grissom's ganglords in one big room—and the Joker at the head of the conference table.

"So that's the way it's supposed to be, gentlemen," the Joker concluded. "Until Grissom resurfaces, I'm the acting president. And I say we start with this Gotham City Anniversary Festival and run this city into the ground!"

All of Grissom's boys muttered to each other. The Joker certainly hoped they all appreciated his efforts. After all, it wasn't as if he didn't have to make sacrifices to run this meeting. First, there was all that trouble finding the flesh-colored makeup thick enough to cover his deadly pallor, then there was the black hair dye over his natural green. Just so he could look like Jack Napier again for this one important afternoon. Of course, there was nothing he could do about his charming new grin, but didn't a big smile make life just that much more pleasant?

The Joker waited pleasantly for the gang's decision. Oh, there were some, like that wimp accountant Luce, that were cowed from the minute he walked into the room. But there were others, like that Vinnie Ricorso over there, who wanted to think for themselves, who actually might question the Joker's decisions.

The Joker allowed himself a silent sigh. Why was life always so full of Vinnie Ricorsos?

"Why don't we hear from Grissom?" Ricorso demanded.

Carmine Rotelli was at the other end of the table. Rotelli was always good at being brave, as long as someone else was brave first.

"How come you're wearing that stupid smirk?" Rotelli demanded.

"Because life's been good to me," the Joker replied.

But that answer wasn't good enough for Rotelli.

"What if we say no?" he demanded even further.

But the Joker was ready for this too. A leader of men had to be ready for these eventualities.

"Nobody wants a war, Carmine," the Joker replied smoothly. "If we can't do business, we shake hands— and that's it."

"Yeah?" Rotelli asked, still a little doubtful.

"Yeah," the Joker agreed. It was time for a demonstration. He stuck out his hand.

Rotelli stood and put his hand in the Joker's. They shook. It was too bad the Joker hadn't told Rotelli about the joy buzzer.

Forty thousand volts surged through Rotelli's body. What was left of him fell back into his chair, smoke pouring from what remained of his sleeves and shirt collar.

The Joker used only the very best joy buzzers.

The doors at the back of the room burst open, and the Joker's own personal army marched in, much more personably dressed than the thugs already sitting in here. Of course, the fact that the Joker personally designed those colorful outfits had a lot to do with their stylishness.

The Joker grinned at good old Bob, his number-two man, as he explained:

"Carmine got a little hot under the collar."

"You're insane!" Ricorso shouted. He looked as if he wanted to leave.

The Joker was quite upset. "Haven't you heard of the healing power of laughter?"

He started to laugh all over again.

"Now, get out of here!" he told Grissom's goons. "And give it some thought."

The Joker's boys escorted the other fellows out. The Joker grabbed a copy of the *Globe* and waved for Bob to stay behind.

"Bob," the Joker spoke tersely, "I want you to take this camera and follow this reporter Knox. Find out what he knows about Batman. You've got to learn to *use* people, Bob."

"Yes, sir," Bob replied. Good old Bob. He always knew exactly the right thing to say.

Bob left. Everyone was gone now, except for the Joker and the charred corpse of Rotelli. Maybe it was time, the Joker thought, for a little conversation.

He turned to Rotelli.

"Your pals, they're not such bad guys. What do you say we give them a couple of days to come around?"

He paused. He had to give Rotelli a chance to reply.

"No?"

The Joker could hardly believe his ears.

"Grease them now?"

Well, if that's what he wanted.

"Okay."

The Joker shook his head. "You're a vicious bastard, Rotelli. I'm glad you're dead."

# C H A P T E R

## Seven

It had to be in here somewhere. WARNER . . . WATSON
. . . WAXMAN was the last folder in the drawer. Where
was it?

A pair of fingers tapped Vicki on the shoulder. She
glanced around, right at a manila folder with the title
"WAYNE, BRUCE."

Allie Knox grinned at her. She grabbed the file from
his hands.

"I'm looking for that." It was a very thin file.

"I thought we were a team here." Knox shook his head.
"I'm losing confidence in you—going out with this
weirdo."

She opened the file. There was hardly anything in here:
"Bruce Wayne Attends Society Fund-Raiser"; "Bruce
Wayne Gives to New Orphanage." This sort of filler
wasn't going to tell her a thing she needed to know!

She had had just about enough. She glared up at Knox.

"You're speaking strictly professionally, right? This wouldn't be a personal issue for you, would it?"

"I just want you to do your job," Knox replied defensively.

"I *am* doing my job!" Men! Vicki didn't know the last time she had been so angry.

"Me too," Knox insisted. "I'm protecting my partner. The guy collects weird weapons from Japan! He probably roller-skates through the female population like a bulldozer."

Vicki punched the file with her fist. "Where does it say that, Knox? There's nothing in this file but social puffery. No photos. No history. Nothing. *That's* strange! Where's he get his money? What's he do all day? *Who is he?*"

She flung the file angrily to the floor and stormed from the room.

"Who cares?" Knox called out after her.

She did, Vicki realized as she slammed the door behind her. She cared very, very much.

She would wait forever if she had to. She had parked a block away from Wayne Manor. Sooner or later, something would happen. She had that same feeling she had gotten sometimes, taking pictures in Corto Maltese, just before all hell broke loose.

Who was Bruce Wayne? If she hadn't been so upset when she first looked at his file at the *Globe*, she would have realized something was really wrong. But she had put it down to sloppy filing at the morgue, or maybe Allie Knox keeping one or two choice pieces for himself.

It was only when she pursued her other contacts—a

sports reporter (once a college sweetheart) who worked for the rival *Gotham Herald*, and an evening news anchorwoman who she'd become friendly with during her years in fashion photography—that she stopped thinking of the lack of publicity as simply strange. Now she thought of it as more of a conspiracy. The *Herald*'s file was every bit as skimpy and uninformative as the one at the *Globe*, full of short news fillers and society clippings. Strangely enough, they didn't have any photos either. But it was the TV station that clinched it. There were no videotapes of Bruce Wayne on file at the station, even though Vicki's friend could have sworn her evening news show had covered dozens of events that Wayne had been a part of.

A millionaire playboy who hobnobbed with the rich and famous every night, and never, ever had his picture taken? That sort of thing didn't just happen. You had to consciously avoid all the "photo opportunities." Even then, someone like Vicki was bound to take a candid of you when you least expected. What could you do then?

If you had Bruce Wayne's kind of money, she imagined, you could always buy the pictures back from some newspaper or TV employee who needed a little extra cash on the side. But why?

Allie Knox might have been right for once. Bruce Wayne was more than a little strange. The more Vicki tried to find out about him, the less she realized she knew, until she was surrounded by a mystery that threatened to consume her.

*Who was Bruce Wayne?* Maybe it had been her pride that had started her on this  but it was her news instincts that would find the truth.

He had gotten too close to the wrong woman. Whatever Bruce Wayne was hiding, it wouldn't stay hidden for long.

Someone dressed in dark glasses and a long black overcoat stepped from inside the gate of Wayne Manor. She thought it might be a workman until she focused her telephoto lens.

It was Bruce, dressed very much unlike a millionaire playboy. He paused to put on a pair of sunglasses, then walked toward the heart of the city, just another working man with a long and narrow package under his arm.

One more mystery, Vicki thought. But this one wouldn't get away. Taking her camera with the helpful telephoto lens, she got out of the car. She paused long enough to lock the door—even in this neighborhood, one had to be careful—then walked, quickly but casually, in the direction Bruce had taken.

She had been following him for half an hour.

A ten-minute walk, and they had gone from the swank area around Wayne Manor to middle-class houses with tiny lawns, double- and triple-deckers, then larger and larger apartment buildings. Another ten minutes and the neighborhood had really started to deteriorate; some of the buildings here were deserted, and there were broken windows everywhere. Trash was piled in empty lots and on street corners. She had never thought before how close Wayne Manor was to this part of town. It was one of the things about living in a big city—you might be living on Easy Street, but poverty was just around the corner.

She walked about three quarters of a block behind Bruce, matching his pace, not wanting to get too close, but keeping him in sight. He never looked around. Whatever he was doing, he seemed totally self-absorbed.

In the last few blocks, some of the locals had started calling out to her—wolf whistles, asking for a date, a few other things that weren't quite so polite. A young woman wasn't supposed to walk alone through this part of town. Still, she didn't think she was in any real danger. They might try for the camera. She kept it half hidden as she walked straight ahead. She doubted they'd do anything else in broad daylight with all these people around. If the worst happened, she'd learned to defend herself in Corto Maltese, anyway.

She had been most worried, at first, that Bruce would hear the taunts and turn around. But he only kept on walking, totally involved in his errand.

Bruce turned abruptly into an alleyway. Vicki hurried to catch up with him, afraid she might lose him if he was out of sight. She recognized this area. They were close to Seventh Avenue, not all that far from the center of town.

She stopped at the corner and took a step back. The alley was a dead end. Bruce stood there, staring at the three brick walls that enclosed him. He looked up at the sky, then over at the alley's far corner. Stepping over torn trash bags and broken boxes, he walked over to that corner. He kicked some cans out of the way to clear a space.

Vicki raised her camera. She'd need the telephoto to get a closer look.

Bruce unwrapped his package. He pulled something out—something hidden by his back. He turned slightly. Vicki saw he was holding two long-stemmed roses.

Vicki clicked the camera shutter.

Bruce knelt, facing the corner, and placed the two roses, side by side, on the dirt and broken asphalt, almost as if he was making an offering to a shrine. He held his hand over his eyes.

Vicki clicked the shutter again.

He stood, and kicked one of the cans toward the mouth of the alley. He was walking back out! It was time for her to vanish.

He didn't see her, hiding in the shadows behind the dumpster. He was still lost in whatever private world had brought him here. He turned down Broad Street, heading for City Square. Vicki resumed her chase, the usual three quarters of a block behind.

When she caught sight of Bruce again, someone was walking next to him. A street mime, with white painted face and outlandish striped costume. Vicki frowned. He was doing one of those mime things—feeling his way along an imaginary wall, she guessed. He wasn't very good at it. She had never much cared for street mimes anyway.

There was a crowd ahead on the steps of City Hall. Bruce hesitated, staring at the commotion. Vicki hurried forward to get a better look, trying to determine what was happening while still keeping an eye on her prey.

The crowd shifted enough so that she could see what was going on in the middle. One of the local ganglords was there—Ricorso, Vicki thought. He was flanked by a couple of overmuscled bodyguard types and a smooth, well-dressed fellow who had to be a lawyer. Most of the rest of the crowd, she realized, were reporters, including Allie Knox.

She looked back at where Bruce had been a second ago, but he was gone.

"So what is this affidavit you've filed?" a reporter was asking. "Grissom *gave* you all his businesses?"

Ricorso glanced at his lawyer before answering. "Mr. Grissom asked me, as a personal favor, to take over the operation of his business until he returned."

"Jeezus," Knox chimed in, "that's a pretty big gift. You must have been very close. Did you do a little time together as children?"

Ricorso sneered as the others laughed.

"I smell fresh ink, guys," Knox added. "I'm sure you can prove all this. Why am I asking? Of course you can!"

Vicki looked around. She had taken her eyes off of Bruce for only a second. She couldn't see him anywhere in the bustling square. She did see an awful lot of street mimes, though. There were at least half a dozen, climbing invisible stairs, walking against the wind, doing all those things that street mimes did. Vicki wondered if she'd wandered into some sort of special event.

She walked over to Knox. There were other photographers here, too. She saw one of them take their picture. Allie nodded to her as she approached. The lawyer was talking now.

"We have witnesses," he said in an official-sounding monotone. "Grissom's signature is perfectly legitimate."

"It's legitimate!" a new voice shrieked over the reporter's questions. "I saw him! I was there!"

Yet another mime pushed his way through the crowd of reporters. This one not only had a chalk-white face, he had added bloodred lips.

"I saw it all," the new mime said. "He raised his dead hand and signed the paper in his own blood. And he did it with this pen!" He reached inside his suit pocket to pull out a quill pen that must have been four feet long. He smiled over at Ricorso as he ripped off his top hat. The hair underneath was green!

"Hello, Vinnie!" he crowed. "It's me, your uncle Bingo! Time to pay the check!"

With that, he hurled the steel-tipped pen straight at Ricorso's jugular. Ricorso fell to the ground, clutching at the thing that had sliced through his throat.

Somebody screamed. Reporters scattered as the other mimes pulled machine guns from the satchels that they carried, guns they fired straight into the air.

Vicki dove behind a parked car. It was Corto Maltese all over again. Knox was right behind her. She looked cautiously back out into the square. There, standing completely still in the middle of the mayhem, almost as if he was in a trance, was Bruce Wayne.

Vicki waved to him as best she could from her hiding place.

"Bruce! Get down!"

Bruce acted as if he didn't hear her. He began to walk, slowly at first, but with increasing speed with every step, toward the mime who had thrown the deadly quill.

The mime laughed, walking the other way. A car screeched to a halt in front of him. The mime calmly opened the door and climbed inside. The car sped away.

The other mimes fled to other cars, and, a moment later, they were gone as well. Racing automobile engines faded in the distance. Somebody was crying. Besides that, there was silence.

Vicki ran from her hiding place.

"Bruce?" she called.

At first, he still didn't seem to hear her. She ran closer. He turned at last. Sweat was pouring from his face. His eyes were two deep hollows, as if he hadn't slept for a month. But it was what was in those eyes that startled her the most—a look of sorrow and fear, like a small boy who had lost everything he ever had.

"I'm sorry, Vicki," he whispered. He turned and ran into the crowd.

"Bruce!" she called again. But he was gone.

# CHAPTER

## Eight

*On The Spot Action News!*

Mayor Borg and that new guy, Harvey Dent, both looked suitably uncomfortable. Oh, they were trying to hide it, but—

The *On The Spot Action News* news-woman shoved a microphone in the mayor's face.

"Does this gang war dampen the city's plans for the two hundredth anniversary festival?"

"The festival opens," the mayor blustered. "The police will stop these gangsters!"

Well. Thank you, Mayor. It was always gratifying to get some recognition.

"Mr. Dent," the *On The Spot Action News* woman continued, "what do you think of the theory that the mysterious 'Batman' is a mob enforcer killing these men?"

*What?*

The television screen shattered as the Joker screamed with rage.

"Batman? *Batman!* Can somebody please tell me what kind of a world we live in where a man dressed as a bat gets my airtime?" He opened the pincers, pulling the giant, retractable boxing glove out of what had once been a television screen. "This city needs an enema!"

He tossed the boxing-glove apparatus to the floor and jumped from his chair, storming out of his newly refurnished lair. Bob, who had just walked in the door, dutifully followed him out onto the floor of the newly remodeled Axis Chemical.

The Joker stopped by a couple of his highly paid scientists. He had to shout to be heard over the machinery noise.

"Have we shipped a million of these things?"

"Yes, sir!" the scientists chorused.

"Ship it all!" the Joker cheered. "Untangle the knots. Roll the wheels. I've got my blood up!"

The scientists put down their clipboards and rushed to obey.

The Joker moved on, with Bob in close pursuit. The Joker banged open the door to his very special room. The room had no windows and very little ventilation. It was in the very bowels of Axis Chemical.

Ah, but what it did have!

The walls were covered with scenes of war, the very best photographs from the very best family magazines. But what was on the table was even better, stacks and stacks of folders, with all those special initials—FBI, KGB, CIA. The Joker especially liked the one on top:

## DDID NERVE GAS—
## RESULTS OF PRELIMINARY EXPERIMENTATION

Stamped across the folder were the words "Discontinued 1977" and "Highly Confidential." But inside was the best part of all—all those glossy eight-by-tens, photo after photo of dead soldiers, their putrefying lips drawn back in very special smiles.

"Losing is a bad habit, Bob," the Joker remarked wistfully. "So much to do and so little time."

Bob stepped forward quickly. "Here's the photos."

The Joker lifted his eyebrows as he flipped through Bob's offerings. He stopped at this photo of a twerp in a polyester jacket.

"Who's this dud?"

Bob glanced over his shoulder. "That's Knox."

"Bad tie," was the Joker's verdict. "No style." He flipped to the next photo.

His mouth opened.

He gasped for air.

His heart went pitter-pat.

"Stop the press! Who is *that*?"

"That's Vicki Vale," Bob answered. "She's the photographer working with Knox."

The Joker licked his ample lips. He needed to study this photo in some detail. "That woman has style! Jeezus Marimba! A lovely beast like that could get a man up and running!"

He pulled a pair of scissors from one of his many pockets and, humming a happy tune, cut the babe's likeness out from all that interfering background. He was careful not to cut too close, of course—you had to leave a bit of a border. What now? Oh, of course! He knew the very thing to do with the border. The Joker reached for his crayons and started to color.

"She's been dating some guy named Wayne," Bob informed him.

"She's gonna trade up!" The Joker leered at the photo beneath his crayon. "Damn!" he added as he chewed on his tongue. "It's so hard to stay inside the lines!"

The border was done at last, a very nice mixture of heliotrope and cobalt blue. The Joker quickly covered the back with rubber cement before giving Vicki a place of honor on his wall.

"I'm gonna get me a new girl, Bobbie!" He took a moment to admire his handiwork, then snapped his fingers.

"Phone book! I've got a mind to make some mayhem."

Vicki Vale, huh? He had trouble taking his eyes off her long enough to find the phone numbers. She looked good in the middle of a war—a war that was going to take all of Gotham City!

The Joker hummed as he dialed. He didn't know when he'd been this happy!

He had had to go home. There was nothing else he could do.

Alfred looked up from his dusting as Bruce entered the study. The butler walked toward Bruce in that quick and almost effortless way he had. He took Bruce's coat, and then, from somewhere, handed Bruce a hot towel. Bruce had given up wondering years ago how Alfred produced these things. Instead, he wiped his hands.

"Miss Vale called," Alfred informed him. "She was

quite concerned." He paused a minute, then added quickly in a confidential tone that Bruce hardly ever heard:

"I've noticed that there is a certain weight that lifts when she's here."

Bruce glanced at his butler. As well meaning as Alfred was, the situation was impossible.

"Why don't you marry her, Alfred?"

"That's not exactly what I had in mind, sir," Alfred replied, still quite stone-faced.

Bruce shrugged helplessly. "I can't go on with this, Alfred."

Alfred nodded his understanding. They'd planned for this too long. They both knew what had to be done. There was no time, now, for a woman in Bruce's life.

"Napier's alive," Bruce continued. "He's running Grissom's men. I've got to find out everything the police have on him."

"Yes, sir." Alfred's tone was businesslike once more. He turned, already headed for the Batcave and the hours of research that had to be done.

Bruce sighed as the butler walked past, a small, sad sound for things that could never be.

"She's good—isn't she?"

Alfred smiled sadly in reply.

Vicki looked at the photos she had taken of Bruce Wayne. When Bruce had disappeared after this, she had stayed behind for a moment to take pictures of the carnage in Gotham City Square. That was her job, after all. But she had developed the roll of film herself, and kept those shots at the beginning that she had taken of Bruce, and the roses, hoping that somewhere in these black-and-white images there might be an answer.

She looked at Bruce, kneeling in the alley. When she had taken this picture, it had almost seemed as if he was performing a sort of ritual. He had been that way in the square, too, in the middle of all that shooting, as if he were no longer himself but were answering to someone, or something, in another time or place.

And she had the feeling that this other guy, the one who called himself the Joker, had something to do with it, too. Bruce had been drawn to that murderous street mime with the green hair, rather like a moth to a flame. She hadn't even known that the mime had a name, until the bullet-riddled bodies of the rest of Vinnie Ricorso's gang showed up on the steps of Gotham City Hall, all nicely wrapped in large red ribbons, with an accompanying card: "A present to Gotham City—from the Joker."

First the Batman, and now this creep. There seemed to be a lot of publicity seekers in Gotham City these days. But how did Bruce Wayne fit into it all?

There had to be something about that alleyway.

She dialed the phone. It rang. Knox picked it up at the other end.

"Allie," she said rapidly, not allowing Knox his usual wisecracks. "I want you to check something for me. Okay? Find out what's so special about the alley at Pearl and Phillips streets. Bye."

She hung up and looked again at the three photos she had taken. Bruce with the flowers, Bruce kneeling in the corner, Bruce kicking the can.

"What's up with you, Mr. Wayne?" she said aloud.

# CHAPTER

## Nine

"And now it's *On The Spot Action News*, with your coanchors, Becky Narita and Peter McElroy."

The camera focused on Becky. She smiled.

"Good evening," she began. "The fashion world was stunned today by the sudden deaths of models Candy Walker and Amanda Keeler. Cause of death has been attributed to a violent allergic reaction, although authorities have not ruled out the possibility of drug use. Peter?"

Cut to a shot of Peter. He smiled.

"—And plans continue for the city's two hundredth birthday as Mayor Borg announced the unveiling of a statue of John T. Gotham, Gotham's founder—"

A hand reached in from offscreen, leaving a piece of paper on Peter's desk. He grabbed the note and read, the smile gone:

"This just in. Three mysterious deaths at a beauty parlor in—"

Becky started to laugh. Peter frowned over at his coanchor. "Becky, this is hardly— *Becky*!"

He jumped up as something crashed offscreen. Somebody switched to a two-shot so everyone could see what was happening to Becky. She was writhing in her seat, her face twisting into all sorts of interesting convulsions. The camera jerked back and forth, as though the cameraman wasn't sure he should be shooting this. Technicians ran in from either side, trying to do something, anything, for poor Becky. She lurched out of her seat, feet wandering this way and that, hands striking out everywhere, sometimes connecting with technicians who had the misfortune to get too close. It was quite an act, but the finale was even better. She began to whirl in a circle, pirouetting like a ballerina, a surprisingly graceful move for someone as spasmodic as poor, poor Becky.

And all the time, she was laughing.

Becky jerked upright. The force of her stopping caused her to do a quite magnificent double gainer over the news desk. And she had stopped laughing. In fact, she had stopped everything. All her muscles were frozen in a death spasm.

The camera showed her happy face.

"Kill the camera!" Peter yelled hysterically. "Kill the—"

The picture disappeared. There was nothing but static.

That was quite nice. The Joker pressed a button. What came next was even better.

The videotape rolled, the Joker's TV signal overriding

that of the news station and every other television station in Gotham City.

The bright, colorful picture showed two cardboard cutouts of those supermodels Candy and Amanda, some hours before their oh-so-unfortunate deaths, waving at the camera. But their mouths weren't quite right. Oh—how clever—they were animated, expanding into two impossibly large smiles!

That's when the cheerful theme rose up in the background:

> "Now spread sunshine all over the place,
> Just put on a happy face!"

The models spoke with their animated lips in twin Betty Boop voices:

*"Love that Joker!"*

Wow. The Joker sighed happily. Was this art, or was this art?

Of course, now it got even better.

The scene shifted to a supermarket, and that most eloquent of pitchmen—the Joker. He wheeled a cart down the aisle, merrily waving to the audience in time to the happy-face Muzak in the background. He grabbed a brightly colored package from the shelves and thrust it toward the camera.

"New, improved Joker brand!" he exclaimed in his best announcer voice. "With my secret sauce—SMYLEX!" His hand pointed offscreen. "Let's go to our blind taste test."

The picture changed again, to show a tied, gagged, and

blindfolded man, struggling—quite uselessly—in his chair. A neat, white title appeared on the lower part of the screen: NOT AN ACTOR

"Oooh!" the Joker's voice cooed. "He's not happy. He's been using Brand X! But with new, improved Joker brand—"

The camera pulled back to show that our blind taste-tester was not alone. Next to him was a blindfolded corpse with the most magical smile!

"I get a grin," the Joker continued, "again and again!"

The camera switched once again to our pitchman, now lounging next to a full-sized cardboard cutout of one of our models once she's had the Joker treatment—that lovely chalk-white flesh, that magnificent green hair!

"That luscious tan!" the Joker announced. "Those ruby lips! And hair color so natural, only your undertaker knows for sure!"

The scene switched to quick shots of a dozen delivery trucks, their sides emblazoned with the names and logos of all the fine products that have made this great nation of ours what it is today.

"I know what you're saying," our pitchman's voice crooned over the pictures. "Where can I buy these fine new items? Well, that's the deal, folks. Chances are, you've bought them already!"

The Joker's handsome and distinctive face returned to the screen. He winked broadly at the audience.

"So if you did," he added cheerfully, "remember, put on a *happy* face!"

The happy voices came back on, singing a different tune: "Joker Brand! We're changing the face of Gotham!"

The Joker cut the transmission. What a wonderful show! He could see all of Gotham now—young women, afraid to get ready for their big night out; young men, fearful of using deodorants or shaving cream; whole families, unable to trust their medicine cabinets.

This was the Joker's finest hour! It was showtime in Gotham forever and ever!

Or at least as long as there was anyone left alive.

Let's see the Batman top this!

Bruce Wayne turned off his television. The Joker's transmission was over. Snow once again filled the screen. It was exactly what he thought was happening. Now he simply had to find the quickest countermeasure.

Alfred entered the room and handed him another piece of paper to add to the file.

Bruce read it aloud:

"Assault with a deadly weapon, age fifteen." He glanced up at Alfred. "Nice guy." His eyes returned to the paper. "Psychological testing—high intelligence, unstable, aptitudes in science, especially chemistry, and art." He made a thoughtful noise at the back of his throat. "Chemistry?"

He flipped to a photo of Jack Napier, then glanced up at his butler.

"Let's go shopping, Alfred."

PANIC GRIPS GOTHAM! the *Globe* headline read. CONTAMINATED PRODUCTS CLAIM 13 LIVES! WHO IS THE MYSTERIOUS 'JOKER'?

An anchorwoman looked out of the TV screen. Her

complexion wasn't very good, was it? And look at those bags under her eyes.

"—six new deaths," she was saying, "with no clues as to the Joker's deadly weapon."

The camera shifted to an anchorman, one with a big, ugly zit on his nose.

"And what is the pattern?" he added. "beauty and hygiene products, cologne, mouthwash, underarm deodorant—"

The camera was back on the anchorwoman. My, she didn't look very good at all. Her hair was all frizzy. She didn't have any eyebrows. You could see every wrinkle on her middle-aged face!

"Or worse yet," she said, "there may be no pattern. The search goes on through Gotham's shopping nightmare."

Gotham's shopping nightmare? My, those newspeople certainly had a way with words, even if they did look like death warmed over. The Joker clapped his hands. This was getting better and better with every passing day!

Gordon couldn't believe the mayor had called him in here. Gotham City was under siege!

Harvey Dent was still on the phone. The mayor started talking anyway.

"We're having this festival if I have to carry a shotgun and get people there myself!"

Dent hung up the phone as the mayor rattled on.

"Do you hear the words coming out of my mouth, Dent? The festival is on! You find out what this madman is poisoning us with, and fast! Do I make myself clear?"

Dent glanced over at Gordon with a If-you-don't-kill-him-I-will look.

"We're working on it," he replied.

Bruce Wayne wandered into his personal armory. Alfred looked up from where he was oiling a blowgun.

"Oh, sir, did you see the message from Miss Vale?" the butler asked. "She'll be ten minutes late in meeting you at the museum."

Museum? Miss Vale?

"Am I—I'm meeting her?"

Alfred nodded in that efficient way he had.

Bruce had forgotten all about it. He hadn't been thinking about anything at all for the past day and a half except this chemistry problem. Was he becoming too obsessed with Napier? But how could you be too obsessed with someone who wanted to kill all of Gotham City?

Still, he had his own life to lead. Apparently, he had promised to meet Vicki at the museum. She was going to be ten minutes late? He was afraid he was going to be even later.

He wondered if Alfred had any idea what time he had been supposed to meet her in the first place.

Oh, he was a clever Joker!

He'd already rinsed his hair a very attractive shade of black. Now he had to cover his white skin with the flesh-tone makeup again. There was no use frightening Vicki Vale too quickly, especially after all the trouble he'd gone to. First, impersonating Bruce Wayne's butler to make the date with the lovely Miss Vale, then getting Alicia—after he'd sobered her up a bit—to call that selfsame butler to impersonate Vicki and make the date on the other end. It probably wasn't necessary to have invited Wayne, but the tidiness of all of it appealed to the Joker. After all, why not kill that millionaire playboy now and get the competition out of the way?

He smiled at his reflection as he put the finishing touches on his face. True, this was all a lot of trouble, but you had to look your best on a first date.

"Jack?" Alicia's slurred voice interrupted his toilet. "Where are you going?"

She staggered into the room, half-closed eyes staring through that white porcelain mask she always wore these days. Such a shame. What could he tell her that her poor, drug-numbed mind could understand? The Joker shook his head. It just proved what too much high living could do to you.

He stood with a flourish, admiring his countenance in the vanity mirror. Was there anything he had missed—any last-minute touch to make the total effect even more devastating? Ah, yes. He placed a very special flower in his lapel. Alicia stumbled back a step.

"I'm going to the Fleugelheim Museum," he announced. "Daddy's going to make some art."

It was hard to pull himself away from the mirror. But he could hardly keep Miss Vale waiting—especially now, when he was perfect.

# CHAPTER

## Ten

Vicki glanced at her watch. She'd been waiting here for twenty minutes! And she was getting angrier with every extra minute that passed. How could she confront Bruce Wayne if Bruce refused to appear?

Why was Bruce Wayne so important to her all of a sudden? They had had only that one night together- -they hadn't made any commitment at all, except for the one that might be in her head.

She didn't know what to think anymore. Ever since the other day, when those two models died right in front of her eyes . . . It was like Corto Maltese all over again, a world full of violence and arbitrary death—a world where you could trust no one and nothing could be taken for granted. She found herself in the middle of a brand-new war, a war where the Joker made up the rules. Except, this time, instead of a war started by a hand grenade or an assassin's bullet, this battle had begun when the two women laughed themselves to death—the Joker's little touch.

Vicki stared down at the gin and tonic on the pastel-blue tabletop. The café here was very nice, on a balcony overlooking all of the Fleugelheim. And yet, it all seemed so unreal here in the museum, her surroundings like a bright, polite coat of paint on the oil-soaked, half-broken machine that was Gotham City. A machine that was about to explode.

It was the fault of Corto Maltese, she supposed. After you've lived in a war zone, you can never quite trust the peace of everyday life. She had lived the last couple of years wandering close to the edge. This time, though, she might have already crossed the edge without even knowing it. What did this madman want from her?

She was beginning to feel trapped. She wanted to talk to someone about all this. She wanted to talk to Bruce.

Somehow, there was an inner strength to Bruce Wayne, something far deeper than the absentminded facade he showed the world. At first, it surprised her how much she wanted to confide in Bruce about this. But her feelings ran deeper than she first realized, and not just about the Joker and Gotham City. Maybe Bruce wouldn't share her feelings, but she had to find out.

She glanced at her watch again. Only a minute or two had passed. She would sit here a while longer. Bruce should be coming. After all, he had reserved a table for them in the museum's tea room. The waiter had shown her there right away, mentioning that Mr. Wayne had yet to arrive.

She started to wonder what Bruce had asked her here for. Unless, Vicki realized, Alfred had arranged the reservation for Bruce. She was rather charmed by the old butler, and she imagined he felt a certain warmth toward her as well. It had never occurred to her before this—Alfred couldn't possibly be matchmaking, could he? If so, what did Mr. Wayne feel about the whole thing? Was that why he was late? Vicki wondered if she might be entirely misreading Bruce's intentions. Why didn't she just get up and leave? She looked at her watch again.

She decided she would wait a minute longer.

She sipped her gin and tonic as she watched a waiter approach. He was carrying a package.

"Miss Vale, this just arrived for you," the waiter murmured before he turned on his heels and disappeared.

It was a small parcel, wrapped in brown paper, with three words written on it in crayon: her name, and a large, red URGENT.

She tore off the wrapper. Inside there was a small, white box, with a note attached, also written in crayon:

DEAR V. VALE
PUT THIS ON
*RIGHT NOW*

Vicki opened the box. But what was this small, red and green thing inside? It looked like nothing so much as a miniature gas mask.

She noticed an odd hissing noise. There was purple smoke coming from the ventilators in the corners of the room. Waiters collapsed on the floor, letting trays of food crash with them. The fellow at the table next to her dropped his fork and fell face first into his pasta salad.

Vicki put on the mask.

A moment later, she was the only one still conscious in the entire restaurant. A hundred people had fallen around her. Some rested on tables, half in and half out of their meals. Far more had fallen to the floor, their arms and legs at unnatural angles. Some of them had collected in piles near the doors as they realized what was happening and tried, futilely, to turn and escape. All of them were out cold.

At least, Vicki hoped they were only unconscious.

The far door of the museum slammed open—violently. Whether she wanted it or not, Vicki was receiving visitors.

A couple of the boys used a little plastic explosive to rip the delivery doors of the museum off their hinges. Sure it was visiting time, and they could have walked right in. But where was the drama in that?

The Joker led the way. He had put on his artist's beret for the occasion. The boys followed quickly, toting the champagne and the glasses, and, of course, Steve-arino carted that huge ghetto-blaster. *Boom, shakalakalaka. Boom, shakalakalaka.* It was time to party.

He walked over to the nearest wall to examine the artwork.

"Okay, everybody," he announced. "Let's broaden our minds."

The boys all went to look at paintings of their own.

*Boom, shakalakalaka. Boom, shakalakalaka*, the radio commented.

The Joker sighed, awed to be in the presence of so much fine art. Not, of course, that these were ideal viewing circumstances. Oh, the champagne and music were fine, but you had watch out with all these bodies on the floor. A person could trip or turn an ankle or something if he wasn't careful. Ah, well. It was true what they said. You had to suffer for your art.

Ah, here was a painting the Joker recognized: "Blue Boy," by Gainsborough, a beautiful full-length portrait of a young man dressed in blue. What lines. What a sense of color. It was almost perfect.

The Joker raised his cane to trace the outlines of the portrait. Yes, he could feel that artistic impulse now. He pressed that special button on the handle of the cane, the one that tripped the switchblade. Now he wanted just the right sensibility here. The Joker bit on his tongue as he carved a large Joker smile in the Blue Boy's canvas face. There! Much better! He smiled at his underlings. Art could be so satisfying.

The boys took that as their cue to make artwork of their own, working quickly with their knives and spray paint, giving all those stuffy old Manets and Renoirs and Degases some thoroughly modern additions.

*Boom, shakalakalaka*, the radio urged them on. *Boom, shakalakalaka*. It was much better with music. As the Joker always said, whistle while you work.

He moved on down the line of paintings, letting the boys have their way with all but the very best. What had we here? "The Scream," by Edvard Munch. A black-and-white figure, screaming with pain and anguish and madness, a creature both pitiful and terrifying in its intensity, as if it contained all the pain and anguish and madness in the world.

Out of the corner of his eye, he saw a dagger swinging into action. He glanced around to see Bob about to make a slice of his own. The Joker raised a cautionary finger.

"I kind of like this one," he declared. "Leave it."

Bob grinned and nodded. He jogged farther along the wall, ready to spray-paint a Jackson Pollock. Jackson Pollock? It seemed sort of pointless, but Bob should have his fun.

In the meantime, the Joker had other business. His date was waiting for him in the café upstairs.

*Boom shakalakalaka. Boom shakalakalaka.*

Vicki could feel the trap close around her.

The Joker and a dozen of his men had burst into the museum and set about methodically destroying the paintings. Vicki wondered if there was some way she could run for it, but, within seconds of their arrival, henchmen were covering both main doors and all of the emergency exits as well.

Then the Joker saw her. He waved pleasantly as he approached. His face was no longer ghostly white, but his unnatural smile was still there. His good cheer made Vicki feel even more trapped than she had before.

The Joker pulled up a chair. He nodded at her mask.

"I think it's safe to take that off."

Hesitantly, she took off her mask as the Joker snapped

his fingers. Two of his goons rushed forward, one with a pair of candlesticks, the other with an enormous portable radio.

*Boom shakalakalaka. Boom shaka—*

The Joker pressed a button. The disco beat was replaced by a thousand and one strings. He pulled a silver lighter from inside his purple double-breasted coat. He flicked it on, and a foot-long flame burst forth. He lit the candles. It was all like some sort of tremendous parody of romance.

"You're beautiful," the Joker remarked smoothly.

Vicki stared across the table. What did you say to a madman?

"Thank you" was what she finally decided on.

"In an old-fashioned sort of a way," the Joker continued. "I'm sure we can make you more—*today*."

He moved his chair a little closer. Vicki resisted the urge to move hers away. There must be some way out of this. She would have to humor him, though, until she found it.

The Joker looked down at a medium sized black case leaning against Vicki's chair.

"This is your portfolio!" he cried in delight.

"Y-yes," Vicki replied, taken aback by his enthusiasm. "I'm meeting a friend who I wanted to see my work—"

The Joker snatched the portfolio and, in a single, fluid move, unzipped it and spread it out on the table. There were fashion photos on top.

"Crap," he announced.

He turned the plastic pages to the magazine covers and celebrity shots.

"Crap," he repeated.

He turned the pages more quickly, past photos of heads of state, world events, scenic vistas.

"Crap, crap, craap!" he reiterated.

The Joker stopped.

"Ah, now *here's* good work!"

Vicki saw that he had gotten to the photos from Corto Maltese.

"The skulls," the Joker gushed admiringly. "The bodies. You give it all such a glow." He grinned up at Vicki. "I don't know if it's art, but I like it."

Vicki didn't know what to say, so she didn't say anything.

"Let me tell you what I've got in mind, sweetie," the Joker began in a voice like velvet. "I was in the bathtub one day when I realized why I was destined for greatness. You know how concerned most people are about appearances. This is pretty, that is not?" He shook his head. "Well, that's all over for me. In crime, the passions ripen fully." His voice started to rise, as if here, at last, was something he really believed in. "Now I do what others only dream of. I do art, until somebody *dies*!"

He raised both his hands in a gesture of triumph. "See? I'm the world's first fully functioning homicidal artist!"

Vicki had had enough of this madman. She glared at him.

"What do you want?" she demanded.

"I want my face on the one-dollar bill!" he exclaimed, the fervor still there.

Vicki leaned back in her chair. "Good goal. I take it you're joking?"

The Joker howled with sudden fury. He pointed at his face. *"Do I look like I'm joking?"*

But instantly the Joker smiled at her again, the sudden anger suddenly over. "Look," he said, the velvet tones reasserting themselves, "we mustn't mistake ourselves for regular people. We're artists! For instance, let me challenge you with a little piece I did." He glanced at one of his men. "Bob, will you bring in Alicia?"

The lackey scurried away as the Joker turned back to Vicki.

"You'll make a pictorial record of my work," he insisted. "You'll be with me in the avant garde."

Vicki realized that, if she weren't so afraid, she might find the Joker fascinating. He was completely mad, and at the same time, completely sincere.

A woman's voice spoke behind her.

"Jack?"

Vicki turned around. The Joker's henchman was leading a woman dressed in white, wearing a porcelain doll's mask. The woman didn't seem to be very steady on her feet, and her guide had to spend as much time ensuring she kept her balance as urging her forward.

"You said I could watch you improve the paintings," the newcomer said. Her voice was slow and unsteady, as if slurred from alcohol or drugs.

The Joker rolled his eyes. "Uh-oh. I'm in trouble now!"

Vicki couldn't help herself—it was the newshound in her. Even though she was afraid of the answer, she asked what was on her mind.

"Why is she wearing a mask?"

"Well, she's just a sketch really," the Joker replied humbly. "Alicia! Come here, have a seat. Show the lady why you wear the mask."

Another henchman pulled up a chair, and Alicia sat. She started to remove the mask. Her drugged fingers moving slowly.

"You see, Miss Vale," the Joker continued, "Alicia's been made over in line with my new philosophy. Now, like me, she's a living work of art."

Alicia took off the mask.

Oh, God.

Vicki lurched out of her seat. She couldn't help herself. The chair fell with a crash as she stumbled away.

"I'm no Picasso," the Joker continued, as modest as before. "You like it?"

Vicki threw a second chair in the Joker's path. Like it? She couldn't look back at Alicia, no matter how much she tried. The left side was perfectly normal, a model's face. But the right side—skin melted into muscle, which in turn eroded away to scar tissue and bone. How long had it taken the Joker to destroy Alicia's face so completely?

The Joker grinned at her, that crazy, sincere grin. What could she say to him? How could she get out of here?

"Uh—it's great," she managed. "But what can I do for you? I—"

The Joker spread his hands wide.

"A little song," he suggested tunefully.

His feet tapped across the floor.

"A little dance," he added cheerfully. He mimed placing something large and round on a pole.

"And Batman's head upon a lance," he concluded brightly. "Tell me what you know about—"

His hands turned into a pair of bat wings.

Vicki shook her head. "I don't know anything about Batman."

"Really?" the Joker replied indifferently, as if this had been the answer he was expecting all along. He wiggled his eyebrows. "Well, then, what do you think about a little 'you' and 'me'?"

This was impossible! There was no way to humor someone like the Joker.

"I think you're insane!" she spat back, half rising from her chair.

"I am? And I thought I was a Pisces!" He spread his hands wide in a gesture of supplication as he stood. "C'mon. Let's make up." He walked around the table toward her. "Here's a flower."

One of his hands encircled a large, purple boutonniere on his lapel while his other hand reached into his coat pocket. The bulb was large and shiny. It looked as if it might be made of plastic. There was nothing natural about that flower.

"No!" Vicki screamed. She jumped aside, almost toppling the table, as a jet of clear liquid sprayed from the center of the purple bloom. A pillar behind her smoked and sizzled where the liquid hit. It was acid!

The Joker grinned at her. He took another step in her direction, as if she would certainly accept the flower, now that she knew its true purpose. He was going to kill her —or worse, make her into something like Alicia. Vicki backed away. She bumped into a waiter's cart. The Joker walked toward her.

She had to keep him away from her. She needed a weapon. She grabbed a water pitcher from the cart and threw it at the Joker.

The pitcher missed, but it drenched the Joker with water.

"No!" He shrieked as his hands covered his face. "No!"

He bent over double. The tan was coming off on his fingers, revealing the bone-white skin beneath.

"I'm melting!" He fell to his knees.

"I'm melting!" He writhed on the floor. "Oh, God, I'm melting!"

Vicki was so frightened that it took her a minute to realize the Joker was quoting the Wicked Witch of the West.

"Help me!" the Joker croaked, staggering back.

Had she really hurt him? Despite herself, she took a step forward.

He leapt forward abruptly.

"Boo!" he screamed.

He was on top of her. She couldn't get away. All she could see was the purple flower, and that big, big grin.

Something shattered overhead.

# C H A P T E R

## Eleven

Everything was perfect until that noise, the Joker thought.

He looked up. Something had come through the sky-light, that same dark something that was dropping to the floor.

No, the Joker corrected himself. It wasn't just any old something. It was the Batman.

He landed only half a dozen feet away. He pointed his fist at the Joker. There was something attached to the bat guy's wrist.

Was Batman going to shoot the Joker? He was too young to die. The Joker considered running, but Batman would nail him before he took a step. Mother of Mercy! Was this the end of little Rico?

The Batman fired.

The projectile split in two, each half embedding itself into the walls past the balcony on either side of the Joker. The Joker realized there were wires attached to each of the spikes, and another wire leading from the Batman to his skylight entranceway.

The Batman grabbed Vicki and swung out along the escape wires he had created for himself, plunging off the balcony and straight through an arched doorway marked "Exit."

It took the Joker a second to recover.

"Those toys!" he exclaimed at last. "Where does he get those wonderful toys?" He looked around at his boys. They seemed every bit as flabbergasted as he was.

"Well, don't just stand there!" he yelled. "Go and *ask* him!"

They went. The Joker sighed. Did he have to think of everything around here?

It took Vicki a moment to realize she had been rescued. Batman had put his arm around her, and, a second later, they were off the balcony and out into Gotham Square. He let her go as they landed, and pointed to a side alley. She ran the way he pointed as he lobbed a small disc into the entranceway behind them. A second later, the foyer was filled with smoke.

"Get in the car!" Batman yelled behind her.

The car? Vicki looked at all the cars parked along one side of the alley.

"Which car?" she asked.

She saw it a moment later.

"Oh," she added. There were a lot of cars here, but there was only one jet-black, supersleek sports car with customized bat hubcaps.

The hood slid forward with a barely discernible whir, revealing what looked more like twin cockpits than driver's and passenger's sides. Vicki climbed into the passenger cockpit. "Ignition!" Batman ordered.

The entire dashboard lit with a dozen different dials and indicators. A small light on the left-hand side flashed "Voiceprint OK." There was some sort of control board between the seats as well, full of lights and buttons and toggle switches.

"Ignition," a computerized voice replied.

The engines revved as Batman vaulted into the other side. The doors lowered to seal them both inside as Batman instructed Vicki to put on her seat belt.

The car squealed down the alleyway, straight toward the doorway they had so recently left—a doorway now full of choking goons.

The goons scattered as the Batman's car roared from the alley. Vicki glanced in the rearview mirror. The Joker's henchmen were climbing into a van and a pair of cars.

She noticed a flashing light to her right. She realized it was a turn signal. She glanced at the glowing speedometer. The car took the corner at fifty miles an hour.

They turned into the heart of Gotham City. Vicki realized with a shock that, despite all that had happened, it was still only early evening—barely after sunset. The streets were full of cars, the sidewalks and crosswalks full of pedestrians. She saw people running as the van behind them careened over a curb.

Batman pushed his car even faster. Vicki saw the blinking right-turn signal a second time. But they must be going ninety by now. Even a car as aerodynamically designed as this couldn't turn at that speed!

Batman flipped one of the many switches on the control

panel between them. A line rocketed from Vicki's side of the car, a line with a spike on the end that embedded itself into a brick wall beyond the sidewalk. The car swung around the corner on the end of the line. Batman flicked another switch, and the line dropped away. They were still doing ninety.

"Damn!" Batman yelled.

They were in a blind alley. The road ended a hundred yards ahead. He jammed on the brakes as he pressed another button on the panel.

As the wheels beneath slammed to a halt, the body of the Batman's car lifted up and rotated 180 degrees, so that it was facing the other way.

Batman pressed the accelerator, and they were on their way again, out of the alley, headed toward Gotham Square. There were orange blinking lights ahead of them—some sort of night construction crew, Vicki realized, working overtime to get the reviewing stands ready in time for Mayor Borg's beloved parade. A gigantic crane was backing down the street into the intersection, blocking both lanes. And they were headed straight for it!

Batman gunned the engine, swerving to the left. There still wasn't enough room. He pumped the brakes as they careened toward the sidewalk. They stopped, inches away from a lamppost.

Pedestrians and construction workers ran toward them, curious about the commotion. Vicki glanced out the back window. The van and the other two cars were gaining on them! She glanced over at the Batman. There must be some way they could get out of here.

"Couldn't we—" she began.

He shook his head. "Too many people." He pressed another button, and the doors whirred open. "Come on!" he yelled as he leapt from his seat.

"Shields!" he ordered as soon as she was out as well.

"Shields," the computer voice replied.

Dark steel plates quickly clanged into place over the cockpit, the wheels, the exhaust system, like nothing so much as an impenetrable black cocoon.

Vicki didn't have time to watch any more. The Batman was already leading her at a run into the construction site. She heard police sirens behind her. Good, she thought. Maybe the cops can slow down the Joker's goons. She didn't for a second think the police had a chance of catching the Batman.

They crossed the construction in less than a minute and turned down another street at a run, dodging openmouthed pedestrians.

An all-too-familiar car pulled out of a side street. Vicki recognized four of the Joker's men riding inside. The goon in the driver's seat picked up a walkie-talkie and said something into it. The car turned toward them.

Batman and Vicki ran the other way. A store window exploded in front of them as the goons opened fire. Vicki dove behind a parked car as the goons' car squealed around the corner.

A little girl, maybe five or six years old, dressed in a ragged, hand-me-down coat, was busily walking her doll around the corner. She was so lost in her playacting that she didn't even seem to notice the bullets and running feet.

She looked up as Batman approached. Wide-eyed, she lifted her doll up so that the masked man could get a better look.

"Is it Halloween?" she asked.

Batman smiled, motioning for Vicki to follow him into an alley. She ran toward him. Her heart sank as she heard the squeal of tires behind her. The Joker's men were back for more.

They drove by the alley, not able to stop in time. But this alley was a dead end too, and this time they had no supercar to save them.

Batman looked up. Vicki followed his gaze. There was a catwalk, but it was five stories up.

Batman looked back at Vicki, the eyeholes in his mask two pools of darkness. "How much do you weigh?" he snapped.

Vicki was a little startled. Even in this day and age, a woman didn't expect that sort of question.

"Uh"—she stumbled—"a hundred and eight?"

He cocked his head a bit to one side, as if performing some quick mental calculations. The bad guys' car squealed back to the mouth of the alley, this time in reverse. They stopped the car in the alley mouth, blocking the exit. The goons piled out of the car.

Vicki looked back at Batman. He was holding some kind of bat-shaped spear gun attached to a thin nylon rope. He shot the projectile aloft. It caught on the catwalk.

He grabbed Vicki around the waist.

"Hang on!"

He flicked something at his belt. Vicki and Batman shot upward, almost as if they were fish being reeled in. A bullet whizzed angrily by her ear. They went up one story, two. But their flight was slowing.

On the third floor up, they stopped. Vicki realized whatever mechanism was reeling them in must not be able to take their combined weight. Vicki felt a mixture of guilt and panic. They were sitting ducks up here. Should she have told Batman how much she really weighed?

Batman twisted around. Vicki looked down and screamed. The goons all had their heavy artillery pointed at the two of them, but the bad guys were taking their time now, waiting for the twisting and turning up there to stop so they could easily kill both of them.

"Whatever happens," Batman whispered hoarsely, "don't let go!"

He detached something from around his waist and hooked it over Vicki's belt.

That's when he let go.

Vicki skyrocketed upward, shrieking as she went. She saw Batman beneath her, cape billowing as he fell the two stories to the pavement. She cried out again as her back slammed against the catwalk. But the rope bounced her up and down a bit, and she realized nothing was broken.

There was a crash beneath her. She looked down to see that Batman had landed in the middle of a pile of garbage cans. The goons rushed over to him. He smashed a pair of them into a wall before he was even on his feet. But a third had found a lead pipe in the rubbish. He smashed it into the back of the Batman's skull.

Batman fell.

The thugs circled closer. Vicki felt so helpless up here. The rope had stopped its bouncing. She pulled herself onto the catwalk, then over onto the roof. But she didn't have a gun. What could she do?

Through all this, she had managed to keep her camera

bag. Maybe, somehow, there was something inside that could help.

She looked down as she unzipped the case.

The lead goon fired two shots, point blank, at the yellow-and-black insignia on Batman's chest. The body jerked.

Vicki leaned over the edge. Was she too late?

The goons stopped.

"No blood," one of them said.

"Jesus," another one answered. "Who is it? Check his wallet."

"Wait a minute," a third interrupted. He crouched down beside the body and poked at Batman's costume.

"What is it?" the last thug asked.

"Some kind of body armor or something," the kneeling man replied.

"He's human after all," the man who had shot him said, courage back in his voice. "Take the mask off."

Body armor? Vicki realized that must mean he was still alive. And she had thought of a way to distract the thugs, and maybe get an exclusive for the *Gotham Globe* as well.

They pulled off his mask, but his face was still in shadows.

"Get out of the way!" their leader yelled. "I can't see him."

That's when Vicki set off the flashgun.

The goons were startled, disoriented.

"Goddammit!" one of them yelled. "It's the girl!"

A bullet *kerrang*ed off the cement ledge three inches from her face. She flashed the strobe again, this time taking a photo as well. She knew she was exposing herself, but she had to get this.

All the thugs raised their guns and fired at once.

\* \* \*

The flashes stopped overhead.

"Did you get her?" a voice asked.

"I think so," a second answered. "Wax him."

Batman opened his eyes as the four gunmen aimed their weapons at him. His right hand snaked up to grab the coat of the nearest one, spinning him around into the gunfire of the other three.

Then Batman was on his feet, using the brand-new corpse for a shield. He heaved the lifeless excrement through the air. The body landed on top of one of his friends. The one who was still alive fell back over a garbage can to crack his head against a wall. He fell down, out cold.

Batman was already on the third piece of slime. He rabbit-punched the slime's throat, then gave his gut a good kick with a steel-toed boot as the thug went down.

Now there was only one more little matter to take care of. Batman pulled his mask back into place as he turned to face his final business.

The last piece of living trash had his gun out, but he was shaking too much to aim. Batman smiled. The trash screamed and ran.

Batman noticed the strobe lights had started again overhead. Vicki Vale was up there, taking pictures.

He'd have to do something about that.


The Batman had disposed of all the goons in a matter of seconds. And then he looked up at her.

She retreated from the edge, so that the Batman could no longer see her. He must know that she had been taking pictures, including some before he had put his mask back on. Pictures that were too valuable to lose. She quickly rewound the film and unloaded the camera. But where was the safest place for the film? Her alternatives were limited. She dropped the roll inside her blouse and started to run across the roof to a door on the far side of the building.

Maybe this was the wrong thing to do after the Batman had saved her life. But there was something about the Batman—something so familiar and so strange at the same time. She realized she didn't want these pictures so much for the *Globe* as for herself. She needed to see his face. Once she developed the film, she would know the true identity of the Batman.

Vicki was gone. He could find her in a minute. For now, there were other things to worry about.

He walked out of the alley and saw the Batmobile two blocks away. It was completely surrounded by police and curiosity seekers. A couple of the cops were actually crawling over the top of the car, trying to find a way in. And there was a gigantic tow truck backing down the far end of the street—the kind of truck they used to haul away tractor trailers—maneuvering to haul away the Batmobile.

The Batman made a snorting sound inside his mask. There were always complications. Oh, well. If he had wanted things to be simple, he would have gone into another line of work.

He pressed a button on his utility belt. The miniature radio transmitter popped into his hand. He pressed the Talk button:

"Shields open," he ordered.

"Shields open," the car's computer voice replied.

The steel plates retracted into the doors and wheel wells.

"Ignition," Batman said.

"Ignition," the car replied.

One of the cops crawling across the hood tried to get a look inside the darkened cockpit.

"There's somebody in there!" he yelled.

The turbine engines revved, and the Batmobile started to roll—slowly at first, to allow the cops to roll off the car and the crowd to disperse, then more quickly as the car pulled free of the throng. The left-turn signal flashed as the Batmobile approached the second corner.

Batman would let the computer drive the car for the next few minutes. He needed the cops out of the way for a while, and the Batmobile made an excellent diversion.

In the meantime, though, he had business that would not wait.

Sirens wailed on the street below. Vicki glanced over the ledge and saw the Batman's customized car tearing down the street, dodging a bus and two taxis, swooping around a gaggle of startled pedestrians. Well, at least Batman had gotten away. Now she had to find a way to get off the Gotham City skyline.

The first door she had tried was locked. That was only to be expected, she guessed, in the big city. But the first roof had connected to a second, with a jump of only a foot or two, and, using an old dining-room chair somebody had left up here, she had managed to climb the five feet up onto a third. And this one had a fire escape that went all the way down. She gratefully started for the ground.

The sirens vanished in the distance. From the intensity of the noise, it sounded as if there were twenty police cars chasing the Batman. She looked down. There was no one on the street below.

She reached the bottom of the fire escape. It didn't quite reach the ground after all—there was a five-foot drop to the pavement below. She'd have to jump. Why didn't people warn you about this sort of thing when you went into news photography? At least, Vicki thought, she was wearing her sensible shoes.

Her camera bag slung over her shoulder, she grabbed the bottom iron rung of the fire escape and swung herself down to the sidewalk. Now, she thought, to get out of here. She glanced quickly over her shoulder. It was too quiet around here. She wouldn't want to run into the Joker's men again—or the Batman now, for that matter.

She quickened her pace, turning her head back to look where she was going. But there was something in her way, something large and black.

She couldn't stop herself. She walked—bodily—right into the Batman.

The breath knocked out of her, she looked up into the masked face.

"Not even a thank-you?" he asked.

Thank-you? she thought. For saving her life? Vicki became instantly defensive, probably because she knew Batman was right.

"Well, I think you might thank me," she retorted. "You were as good as dead."

Batman stared down at her. His face looked so impassive behind that mask.

"You weigh a little more than a hundred and eight" was his only reply.

Vicki heard the sirens again. They were coming this way, fast.

Batman's hands were on her shoulders.

"You'd better come with me," he said gently.

She guessed that she should. The sirens weren't more than a block or two away. She didn't want to spend the rest of her day trying to explain things to the police.

"Where are we going?" she asked.

Batman's only answer was to take her hand and pull her to the corner. He led her out into the street.

She looked up to see the Batmobile screaming toward them. They had to get out of its way!

Instead, Batman stepped directly into the headlight beams.

"Stop!" he demanded.

Brakes squealed. Batman's grip was firm on her hand, keeping her from running. She closed her eyes. When she opened them, the car had stopped, three feet away from her toes.

Batman pointed for her to get into the passenger seat as he leapt behind the wheel. She climbed into the car as the sirens rounded a nearby corner. She could see the flashing lights behind them now. There were at least four cop cars, the closest less than half a block away.

The doors closed overhead, and Batman pushed the accelerator to the floor. The engines roared. Vicki could have sworn she could see flame shooting from the car's exhaust. The car started to move, faster and faster down the broad avenue.

Batman told her to put on her seat belt.

She did just that, glancing over at the speedometer. It looked as if they were doing 140. She looked in the rear-view mirror.

She saw only one flashing light, far behind them. A minute later, even that was gone. They had outrun them all.

They were driving out of the city. Batman slowed the car on a deserted stretch of road bordered on both sides by tall and ancient pines. He flicked another one of the switches on his control console. Vicki suddenly found the window before her had become completely opaque. She couldn't see where they were or where they were going, which, she realized, must be precisely what Batman had in mind.

"This is kidnapping!" she pointed out.

"Looks like it," Batman agreed.

He flicked on a light between them, a light so bright that Vicki could no longer look at him. She blinked, trying to adjust to the brightness, then noticed that she could see out of the front glass on her side again. Not that she wanted to. It looked as if they were driving straight for a sheer cliff wall.

She looked back to the Batman, her eyes finally adjusting to the new illumination. She saw him smile as he hit the gas.

They rushed toward the cliff face.

Vicki screamed.

# CHAPTER

## Twelve

The cliff wall vanished. Vicki realized it was some sort of trick, a projection maybe, something done with mirrors. Instead of smashing on the rocks, the car rushed into the mouth of a giant cave.

Vicki looked overhead as Batman stopped the car. They were in an enormous cavern. Floodlights overhead illuminated the chamber. In places, she could see cave walls of rough-hewn stone; in others, passages twisted their way into darkness. The cavern was so vast that the floodlights could really penetrate only small portions of the overall chamber, making pools of light in a sea of total dark.

She could identify some things in the better-lit corners of the gloom. Over against the far wall was a whole bank of computers, next to a lathe and a jigsaw and rows of tools—a fully equipped machine shop. Beyond that was a table piled with flasks and beakers and Bunsen burners. She guessed it was some sort of chemical-analysis setup.

Vicki decided she wouldn't be surprised if Batman had a whole crime lab down here.

She climbed out of the car as Batman got out the other side. She carefully walked farther into the cave, trying to get a closer look at everything. Batman followed her, keeping his distance. Vicki stepped toward him, into a circle of light.

"Watch your step in here," he suggested. Vicki looked behind her and to her right, the direction she would have walked. Another step, and she would have stepped into a pit so deep that the light didn't show the bottom. She kicked a pebble over the edge. No sound echoed back to her. The pit seemed to go down forever. She looked up. Suspended over the bottomless pit were a pair of gymnast's rings.

"Welcome to the Batcave," Batman said.

There was another sound, far above her, the high shrieking cries of animals. She looked farther overhead, above the gymnast's rings, and saw the shadows of wings in the lights at the roof of the cave.

She shivered when she realized what it was.

"Bats," she said softly. "They're terrifying."

"That's the idea," Batman agreed. He walked over toward the computer wall and a small bird cage, half in shadow, that she hadn't seen before. Vicki followed him over. She realized, as she approached, that the cage didn't contain a bird. It held a small bat with a broken wing, wrapped in bandage and splint.

Batman patted the cage.

"Bats are great survivors."

He moved on to a table, piled high with papers. Vicki

kept her distance from the bat cage as she followed. Behind Batman was a clothes rack, full of hanging bat costumes. She strolled over to take a look. The fabric felt odd between her fingers. It was like no clothing she'd ever seen, an odd combination of natural fibers and something that stretched like rubber, but more than that, too. As thin as the fabric was, it had density and weight, as if the center of the cloth was woven steel.

"What are they made of?" she asked when Batman looked up from his papers.

He shook his head. "It doesn't have a name."

Batman didn't seem the talkative sort. She realized she didn't even know why he had brought her here.

"What are you going to do with me?" she asked point blank, approaching him quickly. She wanted to get a good look at his face. She'd find out something more about him, whether he wanted her to or not.

He glanced at her approach and took a single step away. He was instantly lost in shadow.

"You're going to do something for me," Batman replied.

What did he mean by that? She watched as he walked behind the lab table. Now that she was closer, she could see more than beakers and Bunsen burners. There were cosmetics, deodorants, shampoos—all sorts of products. On Batman's left, a computer printer began to chatter. Vicki looked at a monitor next to the printer, automatically scrolling through an endless list.

"What is all this?" she asked.

Batman turned toward her. His hands, above the table, were in light, but his face was still in darkness.

"The police have got it all wrong," he said brusquely. "They're looking for one product. It's much bigger than that. The Joker's tainted hundreds of basic chemicals at the source."

At the source? Vicki looked at the vast array of cosmetics and beauty-care items spread out before her as she struggled to comprehend exactly what he was saying. "But . . . then whole shipments of every product would be poisoned? We'd all be dead."

He shook his head in the darkness. "No. Each product only contains one component. The poison only works when they're mixed." He picked a can up off the table. "Hair spray won't do it alone. But . . . hair spray and perfume and lipstick will be toxic and"—his hand swept above the drugstore's worth of products—"untraceable."

Really? This was quite a story. Batman seemed to be more than just another guy in a cape punching out bad guys. But, Vicki realized, it wasn't as simple as that. If she wanted to have a real story—one that she could print—she needed to determine his methods, to make sure this was more than speculation.

"How did you figure that out?" she asked.

He didn't reply. He walked away from her again, back into the darkness. Maybe, she thought, there wouldn't be a story after all.

When he turned back to her, he had a thick manila envelope in his hands. He stepped forward and passed it to her.

"Take this to the press."

She looked inside. There must have been fifty sheets of

paper, full of chemical equations and lists of tainted products.

Still, once the doubt had entered her mind, it was hard to get rid of it. She remembered all the rumors and speculation in the news office about who the Batman really was and what he really wanted. These papers all looked very impressive at first glance, but what happened if the science editor at the *Globe* took a look at it and decided it was nonsense? She didn't want to promise anything she couldn't deliver.

"I may have some trouble with that," she said at last. "A lot of people think you and the Joker work together."

Batman's reply was quick and harsh: "Do me a favor. Don't flatter my enemy. The man's psychotic."

Vicki looked up from the papers. "Some people say the same about you."

Batman paused, as if that thought was new to him.

"What people?" he said at last, his voice much softer than before.

"Well, let's face it," Vicki replied frankly. "You're not exactly normal, are you?"

This time, Batman's answer was more confident: "It's not a normal world."

He stepped back as he spoke. He was swallowed again by the darkness.

Vicki suppressed the urge to shiver all over again. The strangeness of her situation seemed to grow with every passing minute. What, really, did she know about this Batman?

"Why did you bring me here?" she asked, hoping he didn't hear the catch in her voice.

He had moved in the darkness. His voice was behind her.

"People need that information."

"But you could have just sent it," she shot back.

Again, there was no immediate reply. Vicki looked around, trying to catch some movement in the total absence of light. But there was no movement and no sound. She could be all alone, lost in an endless cavern.

"You're right," he said in her ear.

She gasped. He stood right in front of her.

"I could have," he added. "There is something else."

Vicki had trouble breathing regularly enough to answer him.

"Wh-what?" she managed.

"You have something I want," he replied.

He took a step toward her. She took an automatic step away. She looked behind her and saw that she was almost at the edge of the pit. How had she gotten back here? Had the Batman maneuvered her to the edge so she couldn't escape?

She looked back. Batman was very close to her. Her hand clutched at her blouse.

"What could I have that you want?" Her voice suddenly sounded very small.

Batman swirled his cape over her.

She felt trapped. She couldn't breathe. She wanted to scream.

His arms encircled her. That calmed her somehow. It was odd. Somewhere, beneath the panic, there was something familiar, even reassuring, about the embrace.

He freed one of his hands and raised his glove toward

her face. There was something in that glove, something acrid. She felt her eyes close. The lids were too heavy to keep them open. It was knockout gas! The panic wanted to rise in her again, but she was tired, too tired. Everything—Batman, the cave, pools of darkness and light—everything was fading away.

The last sound she heard was the flapping of wings.

Bat wings.

She opened her eyes. Sunlight streamed through the windows. She was in her own apartment, in her own bed.

What was she doing here? Batman, the Joker, the Batcave—had it all been some sort of a dream?

She pulled off the sheet and saw she was still wearing the clothes from the day before.

So it was all real. Batman must have brought her here.

But there was something else. Something she had hidden. Something she didn't want him to find.

She sat up and searched inside her blouse. It was gone.

"The film!" she said with a vehemence that almost made the words a curse. "He took the film!"

What could she do? She stared blankly for a moment at the patterns the sunlight made on her floor.

The phone rang.

She reached over to the side of the bed, realizing with the movement that she was still a little woozy.

She picked up the receiver.

"Hell-hello?" she managed.

"Vicki?" It was Allie Knox's voice. He sounded concerned. No wonder, the way she answered the phone. "Are you all right? You want me to come over there?"

"No," she replied with more certainty than she felt. That's when she saw something on the bedside table. "Wait. Allie?"

She picked up the envelope Batman had given her.

"Allie," she asked as she glanced at the bedside alarm clock, "can you still make the evening edition if I bring something to you?"

"Just barely," Knox replied. "Is it hot?"

Is it ever, Vicki thought.

"Yeah, it's hot" was her reply.

"How hot?" Knox insisted.

She hung up on him. Better to get this off to him than to spend the rest of the day in idle chatter.

"Very hot," she said to herself.

# CHAPTER

## Thirteen

WAR OF THE FREAKS! the headline screamed. JOKER AND BATMAN CLASH AT FLUEGELHEIM!

War of the Freaks? What publicity! The Joker had thought it had been perfection itself, until they had brought him the evening edition of the *Globe*. "War of the Freaks" had moved down to the lower right-hand corner, supplanted by a new banner headline:

BATMAN CRACKS JOKER'S POISON CODE!
Citizens Told to Avoid the Following Products!

The TV chattered away with *On-The-Spot Action News*:

"Avoid the following combinations," Peter McElroy read solemnly. "Deodorants with baby powder, hair spray, and Odor-eaters." He went down a list, citing every tried and true combination the Joker had devised, and even a couple he hadn't thought of.

"Safe products are flying in as Gotham City goes on a forced fast," the newscaster continued. "And all of Gotham is wondering what to make of Batman. Friend or foe?"

It was the Joker's turn to scream. Couldn't those *On-The-Spot Action* idiots get anything right? After all the Joker's clever planning, hours and hours putting together the very best designer deaths, those TV fools were wondering about the Batman?

"I have given a name to my pain," he screamed to his roomful of lackeys, "and it is Batman!"

He pulled out a sawn off shotgun and blasted the television screen into little pieces. A few of his lackeys seemed a bit surprised by that. Didn't they know too much television was bad for you?

The Joker leapt to his feet and walked from the room, pushing the door violently out of his way as he entered the factory.

Bob—good old Bob, always there when you needed him—hurried to keep up.

"Bob, you got to possess strength," the Joker began, warming to his subject, "greater strength to inflict greater pain! We've got a Batman to kill!" His hands made enthusiastic strangling motions. "And I want to clean my claws!"

His eyes would no longer focus on the maps. There was only so long, Bruce realized, he could go without sleep, depending on action and caffeine to keep him awake. But there had to be a pattern in the Joker's movements—something hidden in these maps that would lead to his secret factory. If only he could concentrate enough to put all the pieces together.

He glanced up as Alfred put a new cup of coffee in front of him. The butler took a step back, then cleared his throat, a sure sign that he was going to speak his mind.

"Sir," Alfred began. "Miss Vale called again. I don't know what you intend to do about her, but I think your present course of action may just strengthen her resolve. She's quite tenacious."

Bruce exhaled slowly. As usual, Alfred was right.

"I know, Alfred," he agreed, allowing the butler to go about his business. He glanced back at the maps. Maybe he had to get away from them for a while before he could see a pattern—give his subconscious mind, at least, a chance to rest.

Besides, there was something else bothering him.

He had left some unfinished business—something all too fitting with that "millionaire playboy" image he used for a disguise. But he never wanted his disguises to hurt an innocent. He certainly didn't want to hurt Vicki Vale.

And neither Bruce Wayne nor Batman liked to leave things undone.

Who could that be?

Vicki walked quietly to her apartment door and looked through the spyhole.

It was the last person on earth she expected to see—at least at this point.

It was Bruce Wayne.

She unlocked the door and opened it enough for her to see Bruce clearly.

"Well," she said more calmly than she felt, "if it isn't the invisible man."

Bruce offered that little-boy grin of his.

"You saw through me," he replied. He carried a rose in his right hand, and there was a bulging bag strapped to his right shoulder.

Vicki opened the door the rest of the way. She always was a sucker for roses. He handed her the flower. She asked him to come in.

She looked at the rose and suddenly remembered another flower—one that was plastic, and purple, and deadly. So much had happened in the last two days, she didn't quite know how she felt about anything. Like being in a war zone, she thought again. She looked up at Bruce. He smiled nervously.

"So . . ." he began, but he seemed to have no words to follow that with.

Vicki leapt into the silence. It was time for someone to tell the truth.

"Listen, I know we're supposed to ease into this sort of thing, but I'm really perplexed with you."

"Yeah," Bruce replied hesitantly. "I know. That's why I came. I—"

"You lied to me about leaving town," Vicki interrupted. She was on a roll now that wouldn't be stopped. Once she started talking about this, it all had to come out.

"You won't return my phone calls," she continued. And how about his behavior the other day? "Then I saw you march through bullets, like you were trying to commit suicide!"

"Look, I—" Bruce was having even more trouble talking than before. "—I did kind of lose it for a while. But some things just"—he looked down at his hands, as if he

might find the answer somewhere between his fingers—
"affect me."

"Affect you?" Vicki demanded. "You were a totally different person!"

Bruce looked up at her at last. "You have to understand—" He stopped again, as if he had lost the words. "—crime," he added at last. He reached his hand out toward her. "I—I love—this city."

There it was again, the sincerity that had drawn Vicki to him the other night. She still wasn't going to let him get away with it without an explanation.

"See?" she said. "Now he's back—the sweet, caring guy. But you seem to be at *least* two people. Bruce, what's going on?"

He looked away from her, out the window. He bit his lower lip. When he looked back at her, she saw emotions in his face as strong as those he had shown the other day in Gotham Square. There was a new directness in his gaze as well—a determination, she hoped, to set things right.

There was a knock on the door.

Oh great, Vicki thought. The new man in her life finally reaches his great moment of confession, and her apartment becomes Grand Central Station. She smiled at Bruce and shrugged, then walked by him to look through the peephole.

There was a delivery boy on the other side.

"Who's there?" she called.

"Package for Miss Vale," the delivery boy replied in a monotone.

What could it be? Something else from Bruce? If so, he should have timed it to arrive a little bit before he did. Oh, well, she thought, better late than never.

She opened the door and signed for the package. It was only after the delivery boy had handed her the box wrapped in brown paper that she realized it was addressed to her in crayon—like the note the Joker had written to her in the museum.

"Bruce?" she called. "I'm frightened."

Bruce took the parcel from her. Removing his shoulder bag, he marched into the kitchen. Vicki started to follow him, but he shook his head.

"Shut the door," he instructed. "Just in case."

Well, maybe he knew best. "Be careful," she said. "Don't set it off."

She shut Bruce and the mystery package in the kitchen.

What kind of scum would send this sort of thing to a defenseless citizen?

He knew the answer already. There was only one madman crazy enough to send a bomb—or something worse—through the mail. He reached into the hidden compartment in the bottom of his pack. He'd need his utility belt for this.

He pulled the belt free and opened the third compartment to the left of the buckle to get at the ultrasound scanner. It was a neat little device, superficially close in appearance to a stethoscope, except there were twin sonar displays where the earpieces should have been. He ran the scanner over the package.

"What do you think?" Vicki called through the door.

There was no response from the scanner.

"Nothing ticking," he replied.

He pulled a small gas mask from his belt and fitted it

over his nose and mouth. Now there was something he needed from the kitchen. He found a steak knife in the dish drainer. He picked up the knife and gently slit through the brown paper.

Vicki knocked on the door. He jumped back, instantly ready, before he realized where the noise was coming from.

"What's happening?" she asked. "Are you okay?"

He took a deep breath and stepped back to the package, ready to finish his dissection.

That's when the package burst open.

Vicki heard the loud bang even through the door.

"Bruce?" she yelled even more loudly than before. "Are you all right?"

There was no answer.

"Bruce, I'm coming in!"

She pushed the door open.

Bruce stood in the kitchen, staring at the package. A gloved hand on a spring bounced above the box—a hand holding a bunch of dead flowers.

"Very poetic," Bruce said.

He reached carefully into the flowers and pulled free a large white card with lettering embossed in purple ink. He handed it to Vicki.

She read it aloud:

> "Roses are red,
> Violets are blue,
> These flowers are dead,
> You could be too."

She looked up at Bruce.

"He sent something," she said, her voice barely a whisper, "just before he arrived last time."

Bruce nodded his head toward the front door. Vicki realized he was right. They should get out of here. She turned to leave the kitchen.

That's when the front door burst open.

It was the Joker, along with his entire gang.

He grinned at Vicki.

"Miss me?"

He pulled up short when he saw Bruce.

"Well, Miss Vale, another rooster in the henhouse?"

He reached into one of his many pockets and pulled out a revolver with a ridiculously long muzzle. He strode over to Bruce, lifting the muzzle to trace the line of Bruce's cheek.

"Tell me something, my friend," the Joker purred. "Have you ever danced with the devil by the pale moonlight?"

Bruce frowned at the Joker. He wasn't going to try anything, was he? He wouldn't stand a chance against the entire gang. Not, Vicki realized, that they stood much of a chance anyway.

"What?" Bruce said after a moment.

"I ask that question of all my prey," the Joker explained, "before I send a draft through their domes." He chuckled, delighted with his own cleverness. "I just like the sound of it."

The rest of the Joker's gang chuckled along with him.

Vicki glanced over at Bruce. He looked startled for the first time since the Joker had broken in. Vicki followed his gaze.

There was something on the kitchen counter—a high-tech belt of some kind. Vicki had seen a belt like that before. She looked back at the Joker. He was too involved in his own performance to notice anything else.

"Vicki," he wailed, "don't let my happy-go-lucky appearance fool you. I'm really very upset. You were dining with me! Talking art! I was a man who was getting somewhere with a beautiful woman. And then—all of a sudden—without a word of apology, you take off with that . . . sideshow phony!"

He took a step toward her, hands clutched over his heart as he spoke in verse:

> "I'm only laughing on the outside,
> My smile is skin deep.
> If you could see inside I'm really crying;
> You might join me for a weep."

He cupped a hand around Vicki's chin.

Bruce charged toward them.

The fists of one of the gang members got in Bruce's way. Bruce staggered back, sprawling across the counter before he collapsed in the corner.

The Joker pointed his gun at Bruce.

No! Vicki had to do something.

He pulled the trigger.

A red-and-yellow flag popped out of the gun.

"Bang!" the flag read.

The Joker's men thought that was really funny. Bruce cowered in the corner. Vicki realized she must have been wrong about the belt.

The Joker took her arm.

"Come on. I want you to shoot some snaps. Make me immortal." He tugged her toward the door. "It'll be good for you."

One of the gang handed Vicki her camera bag and jacket.

Someone screamed outside the window. Vicki looked down to the street below. A police cruiser had run up onto the sidewalk. Two policemen staggered from the car, clutching at their throats. A woman below screamed again and ran away.

Vicki knew the cause of this. She turned back to the Joker.

"What's wrong with those policemen?"

The Joker considered her question as he, too, glanced out the window.

"Looks like they're rethinking their spot in the social order."

A pair of the Joker's henchmen propelled Vicki from the kitchen. She heard the door slam behind her. She craned her neck around to see what had happened as they hustled her from the apartment.

The Joker hadn't followed his gang. Instead, he had closed the door. He was in there, alone, with Bruce.

They had all turned away! He quickly scuttled across the floor, stuffing his utility belt back in his shoulder pack.

There were footsteps. He looked up. The Joker's obscene smile shone down upon him.

"Listen, Bruce," the Joker said in a confidential tone. "*Never* rub another man's rhubarb! Get me?"

He aimed his gun at Bruce's chest and pulled the trigger. This time, the bullet was real.

# C H A P T E R

## Fourteen

Life was full of its little ups and downs.

The press did have this thing about the Batman. And Batman had stolen Vicki Vale from right under the Joker's pale white nose. But now he had Vicki back again, just the way he wanted. And he had managed to bump off one of her suitors in the bargain, although that Bruce Wayne was an awfully easy kill. Didn't the man have any fight in him? Still, it was reasonably satisfying, the way the force of the bullet threw Wayne against the wall. The Joker had to admit it. He so enjoyed a violent death.

He left the apartment, careful to close the door behind him, and hurried down the stairs. The boys had already gotten Vicki into the van. The Joker leapt in after them.

"Gotham Square!" he cheered. "Lickety-split!"

It was amazing how good a killing could make you feel. The Joker guffawed. From now on, there would be no more downs. Only ups—for all of Gotham City.

* * *

Bruce blinked. He had passed out there for a minute. The force of the bullet must have knocked him cold.

He sat up and examined his side. There was no blood, and no bullet hole. He picked up his shoulder bag. There it was—a new hole, two inches from the zipper. The bullet must have gone through here.

He opened his bag.

The bullet had hit the utility belt, embedding itself into the ultrasound scanner. The scanner was ruined, but he had a couple of replacements back at the Batcave. It had done more than its intended job. Thanks to the scanner, he was still alive.

He was still alive. The Joker's bullet hitting the utility belt—more than that, the exact right spot on the utility belt—some people would think that was incredible luck. But he liked to think of it as justice.

His hands moved along the utility belt until he reached the digital pad. His fingers quickly punched the number. Red lights flashed, followed by a beep. The connection was made. But he couldn't wait, even for that.

He got to his feet. He couldn't start after the Joker like this. But where would Vicki keep something he could use? He ran into the bedroom and riffled quickly through the closet shelves. Nothing was opaque enough, until he found the black ski mask. It would have to do.

He left Vicki's apartment and headed for the roof.

The van was going too fast, even for him. How could you be suave and sophisticated around a beautiful woman when you kept bouncing out of your seat?

He reached forward and grabbed Bob's shoulder—good old Bob—and yelled in his ear.

"Slow down, you maniac!"

Good old Bob seemed to be losing it. The Joker could feel it too. It was getting weird here in the metropolis. Heck, the last time he looked out the back window, he could have sworn he saw a guy in a suit and black ski mask swooping over the intersection on a rope. Was Gotham City going crazy?

The Joker certainly hoped so.

Bob slowed the van to a respectable forty or fifty miles an hour—good old Bob—a quite reasonable rate to traverse Gotham traffic. It finally gave the Joker a chance to place one of his very refined hands on one of Miss Vale's delicate kneecaps. She tried to move away, but the van was too cramped for her to go much of anywhere. Another of the Joker's keys to successful romance, he thought pleasantly: Always corner your romantic interest.

"I'm a little high-strung," he said mournfully—pitifully, really—exactly the sort of tone to appeal to the sympathies of a young woman. "Y'know, I've recently had tragedy in my life. Day before yesterday, Alicia . . ." His voice cracked emotionally. The Joker had to admit —it was a very nice effect. ". . . Alicia hurled herself out the window. She couldn't adjust to my new aesthetic."

He handed Vicki Alicia's porcelain mask, now defaced with an ugly crack.

The Joker shrugged. "But you can't make an omelet without breaking some eggs!"

Vicki looked horrified. Maybe, the Joker reflected, after

they left the van, he should trap her in an even smaller space.

He grinned at her anyway. Just call him a romantic fool!

The Joker's van was down below. It had sped from traffic jam to traffic jam. So far, with the aid of his utility belt and some quick runs across rooftops, he had managed to keep the van in sight. Sometimes you could keep up with the scum if gridlock was on your side.

The van swerved around a mounted policeman. The horse turned around; the cop riding it seemed to have no control over his mount. He swayed back and forth in the saddle and looked around as if he was having trouble keeping the world in focus.

Batman had seen other cops like this since he started to chase the Joker, and still other policemen who were out cold. It was the Joker's doing, of course. But what would the Joker do when he had immobilized all of Gotham's finest?

Batman would have to worry about that when he discovered the Joker's plans. But the villain's van had hit a relatively uncongested stretch of road and was increasing the distance between them. And there was a cop here, about to fall off his horse and possibly hurt himself.

There was only one thing to do.

Batman landed on the back of the horse. The cop turned to look at him, slowly and without surprise, as if having somebody land on the back of your horse was an everyday occurrence. He smiled sadly and shook his head as he massaged his throat. His eyes slid closed.

The cop passed out, the smile still on his face. He started to fall. Batman caught him and eased him from his horse, making sure the cop landed on the sidewalk. It wouldn't do any good to have people sleeping in the street.

Batman glanced at the utility belt, which he had tightened around his suit at the waist. The red light was blinking. Good. Maybe things would be in order again very shortly.

He urged the horse forward. He had a van to catch.

He finally saw the van ahead. He had had to ride almost all the way to Gotham Square to catch up. The Joker's van screeched to a halt a block and a half away, almost colliding with the barricades.

Barricades? He had forgotten. Today was the day of the mayor's big parade—the two hundredth anniversary of Gotham City. Could that have something to do with the Joker's plans?

His horse reared as more brakes screamed behind him. He looked around and saw the yellow Volkswagen. Good. Alfred's timing, as usual, was impeccable.

He dismounted and quickly climbed into the passenger seat. Alfred handed him one of the spare costumes. He immediately started to change. It was a little cramped in here, but he had practiced this maneuver dozens of times for this eventuality.

"Alfred," he said after he had taken off the ski mask, "find the records on my family. I want to check something."

"Yes, sir," Alfred replied. "Be careful."

He nodded as he climbed back out of the Volkswagen, once again clothed as he should be—as the Batman.

He jumped on his horse and rode to Gotham Square.

The junior high school band was playing "Happy Birthday." They weren't playing it very well, of course, which made it even better, what with those red, white, and blue birthday banners flapping overhead. And then the mayor, standing pompously up there on his pompous reviewing stand, along with those other pillars of the community, Dent and Gordon—the mayor started to speak, in that way only the mayor could.

"Happy birthday, Gotham City! You know every city has a father, and no one could have been a better father than John T. Gotham!"

This was just too good! It was time to get out of the van and join the festivities. The mayor went on, in that way the mayor did, about all the wonderful attributes he imagined Gotham City had. The Joker made sure that Bob—good old Bob—brought Vicki along. After all the inconvenience they'd put her through, he didn't want her to miss all the fun.

The Joker and his boys pushed their way through the crowd. The mayor waved his flabby hands at the canvas-covered statue at the platform's side.

"I dedicate this statue," the mayor continued in that continuing way of his, "of a man who embodies the past, present, and future of our great city."

Could this be any more perfect? The Joker almost wished he could make some noise, but he wouldn't want to distract anyone from the ceremonies.

The mayor pulled the cord. The canvas dropped away.

What? Imagine the Joker's surprise. It wasn't a statue of John T. Gotham after all. No, this statue's subject was much more handsome—well, actually, the Joker had no idea at all what John T. Gotham looked like, and, what's more, he really didn't care—not when you had a magnificent statue like that to look at! There it was, in the finest Gothic postmodern neorealistic expressionistic style—the Joker!—waving a lovely pair of Uzis just like they were six-shooters. What a sense of style! What finesse! Here was a piece of art that really spoke to you!

The Joker couldn't have been prouder if he'd sculpted the thing himself. Which, after all, he had.

He turned to Vicki. Bob—good old Bob—had made sure she was holding her camera.

"Start shootin', my sweet," the Joker yelled as he took the stage. "I'm makin' history!"

"Sorry!" He waved apologetically to the crowd as he stepped up next to the mayor. "No autographs!"

The mayor appeared less than pleased to see him. Maybe it was because the Joker had switched the statues. Or maybe it was because the Joker was holding a real Uzi pointed at the mayor's belly. Whatever his problem was, the mayor just didn't want to give the Joker the microphone. The Joker had to take the mike for himself.

"C-call the police!" The normally verbose mayor seemed to have lost his way with words. Perhaps the Joker could help him along.

"What police?" he asked sweetly. He waved at the policemen, unconscious on the sidewalk, and more policemen, equally unconscious on the grass, and even more policemen, completely out cold at the base of the statue. The mayor stared, goggle-eyed, at his entire police force, lying down on the job! Poor Borg. That sort of thing seemed to take away his voice entirely.

Well, someone had to pick up the slack here. Thousands, maybe tens of thousands, of city dwellers had shown up for this little celebration, and the Joker wouldn't want any of them to get bored. Heavens forfend! If they left now, they would miss the parade!

The Joker smiled out over the crowd—his crowd. As their beloved mayor had said as he unveiled his handsome statue, he was the past, present and—most certainly—the future of Gotham City, whether they wanted him or not! This was his moment of triumph!

Ah, but triumph was no good unless you shared it with someone. He spoke into the mike:

"Hi, there, fellow Gothamites! As the *next* founding father of this fair city, I declare these celebrations well and truly open!"

He raised his Uzi into the air and fired a quick burst of bullets in celebration. Overhead, half the banner shook loose, riddled by bullet fire. Oh, dear. Clumsy, clumsy Joker. Give him a gun, and see what he does?

The Joker laughed, loud and long. This was the best time ever!

But something else was going on, down in the crowd. People were screaming—Come on now! Don't be impatient! That isn't supposed to happen until later!—and pointing up toward the roof on the far side of the square. Roof? Who did the Joker know in high places?

That's when something came hissing through the air to

wrap itself around the head of the statue—the Joker's statue! It looked like one of those things they used in South America—bounco, bilbo, it was on the tip of the Joker's tongue—bolo, that's what they called them, made of two balls attached by a rope. Except, in this case, the hissing noise was coming from the balls! That meant it had to be a bolo bomb!

The crowd was screaming and running away. Just when the Joker was warming up, too! And the Joker knew the creep responsible for this, even before he saw him on the rooftop.

It was the Batman.

*Now?*

Boy, that guy sure knew how to spoil a party!

That's when the bombs went off. Nice explosion. And when the smoke cleared . . .

The Joker head was gone.

"My very face," the Joker whispered. "Destroyed." He had to admit it. Batman's toys had come through again. He was impressed.

His boys opened fire on the Batman. The bullets didn't seem to do any good. Batman shot out a couple of those ropes he was so fond of using, and swung down to the ground between them. The Joker's boys attacked Batman with their fists. He kicked them aside and headed for their boss.

Oops! The Joker decided it was time for Plan B. When the fancy stuff didn't work, you went back to the bad-guy basics—threats, violence, murder. You know, the traditional values.

The Joker grabbed the mayor.

## Fifteen

Batman was here!

Vicki wanted to yell out loud. She might have, too, if the Joker's gang wasn't still surrounding her. She had kept her cool until now, looking for a chance to escape somehow before the Joker had her disfigured or killed. But they had watched her too closely. There had been no chance of doing anything—until now.

The Batman stood on a rooftop across the street. He fired a pair of lines into the grass of Gotham Square and swept down between them, landing only a dozen feet away. The Joker's goons tried to stop him, first with their guns, then with with their bodies and their fists. Batman got by them as if they weren't even there.

That's when the Joker grabbed the mayor. He stuck his revolver against Borg's temple.

"Damn!" he yelled cheerfully. "I got a good one for you, Batman. What's red and bloody and has no brains?"

Batman didn't answer him. He stepped toward the Joker instead. Mayor Borg was sweating and sputtering. The Joker jammed the muzzle tighter against the mayor's skull.

It looked like the Batman didn't care what the Joker did. He vaulted up onto the stage and started to walk behind the Joker. The Joker swung the mayor around so that he could watch his adversary's moves.

"I didn't know bats came out in the daytime!" he called.

The Batman stopped his circling. He stood staring at the Joker, every muscle knotted and tense, as if he was about to explode.

"Just when murderous clowns leave the circus," he replied. "Let the mayor go."

"Aw, can't I keep him?" the Joker whined. "I'll feed him! Honest!"

Batman wasn't particularly impressed by the villain's sarcasm.

"What do you want from this city?" he demanded.

The Joker looked skyward for an instant, as if lost in thought.

"I want a new bicycle . . . ," he began slowly. "I want to visit Florida. . . . I want—"

This had gone far enough. Vicki had stood here too long as the helpless observer. There was something else she could do—something the Joker had even asked for.

She raised her camera.

"Let me get this, Joker."

The Joker swiveled both himself and the mayor around for the best possible photo opportunity. Vicki took the picture with the brightest flash gun she had.

Batman snapped his fingers.

"Joker!"

The Joker looked back at him. The Batman was less than three feet away. Somehow, in the instant it had taken Vicki to snap the photo, Batman had crossed the stage. He waved one of his gloved hands. There was something in it—a playing card.

A joker card.

Batman punched the madman in the face as the Joker stared. The mayor fled as the Joker staggered back. He shook it off in an instant, turning his stagger into a dance as the rest of his goons lost themselves in the crowd. Finally, well clear of striking distance, he stopped and grinned at the Batman.

"The odds are even!" he declared. "So I'm a-leavin'! You got your toys—I got mine!"

He jumped onto the statue platform and was instantly surrounded by great plumes of colored smoke. A dozen roman candles flew from the smoke, ascending into the heavens. Batman started for the statue, but stopped before he was halfway across the stage. He knew, Vicki realized, by the time he could reach the statue, the Joker would be gone.

Instead, Batman moved for the corner of Gotham Square, where the Joker had left his van. The goons piled in and took off before he could get off the stage.

Vicki lifted her camera again to take a close-up of the Batman.

"Thanks," he told her.

"So we're even," Vicki replied. "I don't owe you anything."

"Whatever you say," Batman replied neutrally.

What did he mean by that? It was impossible to tell. There was no way you could read somebody's emotions when half their face was covered by a mask.

Still, maybe she shouldn't have talked about "being even." She didn't realize, until she'd blurted that out, how guilty she still felt about what she had done after the first time he had rescued her. If that's all she felt about the Batman. Maybe the Batman wasn't trying to tell her anything at all. Maybe she was trying to tell herself something about the Batman.

It had taken her only a moment to think of all this, but, in that moment, the Batman had shot another line aloft and disappeared, back onto the roofs. Vicki quickly took a photo of his disappearing form.

That was her job, after all.

"And you didn't have film in the camera?"

She felt bad enough without Allie Knox rubbing it in. She had been under a little duress, after all. But they would have been great shots—no one had gotten a really good close-up of the Batman before. In fact, they still hadn't gotten a good close-up. It was the kind of mistake a film student would make. She felt terrible about it. How could she explain?

"This goon handed it to me" was the way she tried. "I didn't check." How could she tell Allie how shaken she had been, first from the excessive attentions of the Joker, then from the cold reaction of the Batman? She decided she couldn't.

"Oh, Allie, I'm really losing it" was what she said

instead. She sat heavily on the edge of the desk and stared down at her shoes.

Allie took pity on her and didn't pursue it any further. Instead, he patted her on the shoulder.

"I found out about your strange street corner," he said softly.

She looked up at him.

"Your friend, Bruce, is pretty screwed up," he added, a touch of apology in his voice.

Oh, great. This was all she needed to hear.

"More good news?" she asked without much enthusiasm.

He waved to her to follow him across the office, to the microfilm reader. She stood and slowly crossed the room to stand behind him as he twirled the knob on the side of the machine, searching for the proper page.

"Okay," he said at last. "Here we go." He stepped out of the way. "Check it out."

Vicki stared at the screen. This time, Knox had found something important. It was the front page of the *Gotham Globe*, twenty-odd years ago. A banner headline screamed across the front page:

### THOMAS WAYNE MURDERED!
Prominent Doctor, Wife Slain in Robbery
Unidentified Gunman Leaves Child Unharmed

But it was the photograph beneath that headline that told the real story. A pair of cops leaned over a pair of corpses. Behind them, medics stood with stretchers. But off to one side was a young boy, maybe ten years old, his arms wrapped around the waist of another cop. The boy, Vicki realized, was Bruce Wayne. But it was that look on his face—a wild look, full of anger and despair, as if he had gotten a glimpse at the end of the world—that struck her. It was the same look she had seen on Bruce's face the other day in Gotham Square.

"Some snap, huh?" Knox's voice pulled her from her reverie.

"Oh, my God," she said, finding her voice. "His parents were murdered in that alley. That's why he went there." She glanced up at Allie before she turned back to Bruce's photo, drawn to the frightened boy. "It was the anniversary of their death."

"Yep," Knox agreed, looking at the screen over her shoulder. "Poor kid watched the whole thing happen."

"Allie," she replied, as if speaking the words aloud might force some reason out of them, "the look on his face, it's just like that day with the Joker, in front of City Hall."

But why? she asked herself. Could it have been the sudden violence, bringing back the memories? Or was there more than that?

"Can you imagine what this could do to a guy, Vicki?" Knox asked. For a change, there was genuine sympathy in his voice.

She could imagine, but she wasn't going to tell Allie everything just yet. This could explain a lot about Bruce's behavior. She remembered seeing that odd belt on the kitchen table. She had been so happy, too, in that moment when she had rushed home from Gotham Square, to find that the Joker hadn't left a corpse behind.

But there had been no sign of Bruce since—no note, no phone calls, no assurances that he was fine, or any questions after her welfare. Why?

She realized this photo might explain more than just Bruce. She remembered a talk they had had, at Wayne Manor, about finding your true purpose in life.

"Allie," she asked slowly, trying to keep the question as neutral as possible, "does it say how old the father was . . . when he was killed?"

Knox nodded, like it was the most natural question in the world. "Yeah. I noticed that, too. He was a young guy—just turned thirty-five."

Thirty-five? Bruce was thirty-five. All her doubts left her. It had to be.

She grabbed her coat and camera bag.

"I've got to go."

She backed out of Allie's office.

"Okay!" Knox smiled affably and waved good-bye. "Don't let your personal feelings interfere with your job!"

Poor Allie. He was still playing the wounded suitor. It was much too late for that.

Vicki just hoped it wasn't too late for Bruce.

Bruce woke suddenly.

He had fallen asleep on the map of Gotham City. He had been staring at it, hoping somehow that the maze of streets and buildings would somehow open up to show him the Joker. He looked up. Thirty video monitors looked back at him, showing thirty empty rooms. There was the slightest of noises behind him. He quickly glanced back. Alfred was quietly folding the cape of his uniform.

That meant the butler must have brought what he asked for.

"The file on my parents?" Bruce managed.

Alfred solemnly nodded toward a manila folder on the corner of the desk. Even half asleep, Bruce noticed the butler was unusually quiet.

"What's on your mind, Alfred?"

"I'm getting old, sir," the butler replied. "And I don't want to fill my days grieving for old friends. Or their sons."

Bruce conceded that Alfred had a point. But it was far too late to change his course of action now. It had probably been far too late on the day his parents died. There was only one thing he could do—one real reason that the Batman had come into existence—and the Batman had to fulfill his destiny.

Bruce asked Alfred if he might have some coffee. He opened the file.

They had the press conference on the steps of Gotham City Hall. That in itself was significant. Yesterday, Commissioner Gordon knew, Mayor Borg would have led any press conference from the newly built reviewing stand across the street in Gotham Square. The mayor wanted that stand, and the celebration surrounding it, to begin a renewal of all that was good about their city.

But the Joker had changed all that. His murderous actions had instead turned the reviewing stand into a symbol for crime and anarchy—all the things that were wrong with Gotham. And, in a way, even though the Batman frightened him off, the Joker could claim a victory.

Tomorrow, the city would tear that podium down.

Borg cleared his throat and spoke into the dozen microphones on the stand before him.

"The two hundredth anniversary birthday gala has been indefinitely postponed."

That's all the mayor could bring himself to say. He stepped aside and let Harvey Dent—the new voice of Gotham City—take center stage. Commissioner Gordon never thought he would see the day when Mayor Borg could not talk forever about whatever glory or tragedy had affected Gotham. But this renewal of the city had been the mayor's personal fantasy, something he could leave behind for posterity and the history books. Failure here pointed to the failure of his whole political career. For the first time since he had shared political office with Borg, Gordon realized, he actually felt sorry for the mayor.

Dent looked straight into the central television camera and began to speak.

"We're vehemently opposed to terrorism in any form. But a toxin has been found in the coffee at the police stations. With two thirds of our police force disabled, we simply can't guarantee public safety—"

Dent hesitated. Somebody had run out of one of the mobile video trucks and was yelling at the cameramen. Gordon glanced over at the mayor. Borg started to whimper. The commissioner ran down the steps to see what the problem was. He joined a group of technicians clustered around a monitor.

"What's going on?" he demanded.

"See for yourself," a thin, balding fellow replied. "This monitor shows the feed going out to the local stations. But only one half of that picture is ours."

Gordon looked at the monitor for himself. The screen was split down the middle, with the left half showing the scene at City Hall. The right half was blank, showing nothing but video snow. But then a picture formed in the snow, and solidified to show the figure of a man sitting in an armchair in a drawing room.

Gordon recognized the figure in the chair only when the picture came into focus. It was the Joker.

"Joker here."

The Joker smiled convivially. Rather than a bizarre combination of dead white and flaming red, his face was a neutral flesh color. It almost made him look human.

"Now," he continued, his tone slightly chiding, "you guys have said some pretty mean things. Some of which, I admit, were true under that fiend, Boss Grissom. He was a terrorist and a thief. But, on the other hand, he was great at bridge. Anyway, he's dead, and he left *me* in charge."

The Joker paused and leaned toward the camera. "Now, I *can* be theatrical, maybe even a little rough. But there's one thing I'm not. I'm *not* a killer. I'm an artist."

He leaned even closer, so that his grin filled the screen.

"And I *looooove* a party! So, truce, guys!" The camera retreated as he spread his arms wide. *"Commence au Festival!"*

His announcement was greeted by applause. Canned applause.

"I even got a little present for Gotham City!" the Joker continued, his voice rising with the excitement. "At midnight I drop twenty million dollars cash on the crowd!"

He waved his hands again, this time as a gesture of humility.

"I've got plenty," he added, "so don't worry about me."

The mayor had taken the microphone back on his side of the screen.

"We are not prepared to discuss any deals—" he began.

"You heard me, folks!" the Joker interrupted. "Twenty million dollars!"

The Joker stood, placing his thumbs behind the lapels of his double-breasted suit coat.

"And there will be entertainment!" he cheered. "The Big Fight! Me in one corner, and, in the other, the man who has brought the real terror to this city." He paused dramatically, his eyes wide with feigned fright. "Batman!"

The left-hand side of the screen showed Borg and Dent glance at each other in surprise.

The Joker leaned into the screen.

"Can you hear me, Batman?" he asked in a stage whisper. "Just you and me. *Mano a mano!* I've taken off my makeup. Let's see if you can take off yours!"

Bruce shut off the TV. He had seen enough. He went back to the police file—the one on his parents. The cover had a large blue stamp across it—"UNSOLVED."

But it wasn't, not anymore.

The first thing in the file was the newspaper article, and the picture of Bruce as a boy.

He remembered. There had been a radio playing some-where. It was a hot summer night. A woman laughed, the sound drifting down from a second-story window. He was walking with his mother and father, down the streets of Gotham City. It was a special night. They had been to see a show, and Bruce had been allowed to stay up well past his bedtime. It was such a fine night, his father had decided they should walk for a bit before they got a cab.

He remembered the quick footsteps behind them. He remembered his mother's hushed voice next to him.

''Tom, there's someone following us!''

Somehow, the three of them had started running. But they stopped when they ran into the alley.

He remembered the two young hoods. One of them had a gun. He grabbed the string of pearls around his mother's neck. His father tried to grab the young punk's arm.

There was a gunshot.

He remembered his father falling. He remembered his mother screaming.

A second gunshot.

He could still see the fire from the muzzle of the gun, so bright in that dark alley. And he saw his mother fall. Dead.

Both his mother and father were dead.

He remembered.

The kid without the gun ran away. But the other one pointed his revolver right at Bruce.

''Tell me, kid,'' the kid with the gun had started. He remembered that too.

The young punk stepped forward, so that Bruce could

see him better in the moonlight. He smiled. Bruce remembered that smile. A Joker's smile.

The punk spoke: "You ever danced with the devil by the pale moonlight?"

The young Jack Napier's finger pressed lightly on the trigger.

Nothing happened.

"Come on!" a voice yelled out of the darkness. It was the voice of the other punk, Bruce realized now.

"Let's go!" the other voice insisted.

Jack Napier walked slowly from the alleyway, laughing all the time.

Bruce remembered the laughter.

Alfred let Vicki in.

Bruce was there, asleep in an overstuffed chair. He looked as though he was having a nightmare. His head tossed from side to side, face covered with sweat. He moaned softly, the noise coming from deep in his throat. Vicki wondered if she should try to wake him up. She took a step toward the chair.

His eyes snapped opened.

"It was *him*!" he said clearly.

Vicki walked quickly to his side.

"Are you all right?"

He blinked at her, disoriented, as if he wasn't completely awake.

"Wh—how did you get in here?" he managed blurrily.

"Alfred," Vicki replied. The butler nodded to her as he left the room. It had seemed so simple on the way over here. There were things that had to come out in the open now, for Bruce's sake, and for both of them.

She had to say it now, or it would never come out.

"Am I crazy?" she began. Once she started, the words came pouring out. "That wasn't just another 'night' for either of us. Was it? We got to each other. Didn't we?"

Maybe she was going too fast. Was she making sense?

Bruce closed a folder that had been spread on the table before him. One word, "UNSOLVED," was stamped in blue on the cover. He sat up in his chair and looked directly at her.

"You were going to tell me something at my apartment," she asked, fumbling a bit under Bruce's gaze, "when the Joker came. What was it?"

Bruce looked away. But she wouldn't let him go. Not now, not after all this. Why wouldn't he understand?

"Why won't you let me in?" she asked.

He stood up then, in a quick, fluid movement, as if there was something inside him that his muscles could no longer contain. His eyes looked back into hers. Maybe, Vicki realized, he understood after all.

"You got in already," he replied.

My God, Vicki thought. Is he saying what I think he's saying? She had prepared all these answers for him, all these reasoned arguments for all the objections he could throw against her.

The only thing she wasn't ready for was what he had just said.

"I don't know what to think about all this," she confessed.

"You said you got to a place where you just had to live with the way you were." He waved his hands outward, from himself to the room around him. "Well, that's this place."

She wasn't sure if he meant all of Wayne Manor, or what was going on inside his own head. In a way, she supposed, he could mean both.

Who would be the first person to talk about it, then? To live with the way you were. It was strange, Bruce being so open like this. She had to be open with him too—as open as she could be.

"I've loved you—every night—since I met you," she said. "But I don't know if I can love you dead."

So she had talked about it in a way—Bruce's other self. But she still hadn't mentioned the name.

Batman.

Still, Bruce knew exactly what she meant. "I can't help you out with that." He took a step toward her, then stopped again. "I've been trying to avoid this. But that's the way it is." His mouth twisted up into the faintest hint of a smile. "I wear a cape. You take pictures. It's not a perfect world."

"It doesn't have to be a perfect world," Vicki replied quickly, realizing, in a way, that Batman was beside the point. "I've just got to know if we're going to try to love each other."

Bruce stood there and looked at her. Vicki realized that through this whole conversation they had still kept their distance. Why were they so afraid of touching?

Maybe it would make this all too real.

"He's out there tonight," was all Bruce would say to her. So, even now, he was thinking about the Joker. "Now I've got to go to work."

He left her with a smile, retreating to the shadows at the far end of the study. She heard a door open and close.

She was alone.

What had happened here?

She thought about what Bruce had said—about this not being a perfect world.

She was a photographer. She kept life at a distance in a way. She controlled her surroundings by what she chose to see through her camera lens.

In a way, Bruce did the same thing. He took on a new identity to control his surroundings, except that his surroundings were a lot more violent, because, perhaps, of what had happened to him so long ago.

She wasn't worried about Bruce anymore. Oh, she was still afraid for his physical safety, especially with someone as crazy as the Joker. But she understood why he had to be the Batman. And she hoped he could accomplish everything he set out to do.

She took a sip from her neglected drink.

Just come back to me, Bruce. Now that they had found each other, two crazy people in a crazy world, maybe they could make the world work for them.

And maybe they could even learn to live together in a world that was all too real.


The Joker was Jack Napier.

Batman could no longer remember the moment he made that realization. He had been poring over the maps and police files, or he had had a dream. He had been in the Batcave, or dozing in his study. He had been only half awake for the longest time, really. Now, that he had the answer, everything fell into place. He no longer needed to sleep. All his fatigue was gone, his weaknesses forgotten.

It was nighttime. Bats went out at night.

He put on his gloves, his boots, his cape and cowl. Then his belt, a brilliant yellow oval surrounding the emblem of a bat.

The Joker had challenged him.

Tonight he would meet that challenge.

He climbed into his car and headed for the Axis Chemical Company.

# C H A P T E R

## Sixteen

He was patient.

An unmarked panel truck drove to the gates of the Axis Chemical Company.

He was about to be rewarded.

The gates opened. The truck passed through.

He turned on the headlights and stamped on the accelerator.

The Batmobile roared from the darkness.

The hood in the guard's uniform tried to close the gate again. But the Batmobile smashed its way through the steel bars before they could lock as the hood jumped out of the way.

"It's Batman!" the guard screamed.

It was nice to be recognized.

The guard took out his pistol and shot at the car. The bullets bounced off the Batmobile's steel frame.

He had stopped in front of a pair of large steel doors—the main entrance to Axis Chemical.

He opened the Batmobile's flaps, then pressed a second button to position the heavy duty machine guns. Time for the third button—the red one.

The guns fired, demolishing the steel doors.

He saw the guard from the gate run away.

He flicked another switch, and the guns retracted into the body of the car. He drove the Batmobile through the new opening, into the Axis Chemical Company.

He saw a dozen or more punks running for cover. They opened fire on the Batmobile with machine guns. There were too many bullets. There were already cracks forming in the bulletproof glass of the windshield. If enough bullets hit the glass, it would shatter.

He put up the shields.

The punks kept firing. He'd let them. Their bullets couldn't do any more damage now.

He flipped another switch on his control panel.

The robot arms extended themselves from the hubcaps, each arm holding a sufficient quantity of plastic explosive. He instructed the arms to stretch to their limits and to deposit their loads in a circle around the Batmobile.

He flipped the red toggle switch. A red number flashed on the digital display: 15.

Then: 14—13—12—11—10—9—8— 7—6—5—

He stopped breathing.

The monitor display changed to a single word: DET-ONATE.

The building detonated—a ball of fire rising into the night sky.

He waited a moment for the debris to settle, then drove the Batmobile out of the rubble and back to the gate.

He walked out of the darkness and patted the Batmobile on the fender. There were a couple of nicks on the windshield. Besides that, he couldn't see a scratch. He put the remote control into its compartment on his utility belt. The Batmobile purred beside him.

There was a loud, chugging sound as a helicopter rose from behind one of the Axis Chemical buildings not demolished by the blast. A dozen searchlights came on, all pointed at the Batman. He jumped around the Batmobile, behind the steel gate, as he was surrounded by machine-gun fire.

The chopper roared overhead.

"Not even close!" the Joker's voice screamed from a loudspeaker above. "No cigar, fool!"

His chuckle echoed through the machine-gun fire. "I'm going to the festival. You really ought to show up. I'm gonna kill a thousand people an hour until you do!"

The Joker started laughing again as the chopper banked away from the Axis Chemical Company and headed for the searchlights of the Gotham City Festival.

Laughter.

*Have you ever danced?*

Laughter Batman had heard before.

*Have you ever danced with the devil?*

Laughter he had heard in his dreams.

*Have you ever danced with the devil by the pale moonlight?*

Laughter he swore he would never hear again.

\* \* \*

Such a peaceful night in a Gotham City warehouse. The night watchman—the only night watchman in the whole, peaceful warehouse—sat reading one of those lurid tabloid newspapers. PYGMY FLYING SAUCERS LAND IN RUSSIA! GHOST OF ELVIS LOSES 60 POUNDS ON MIRACLE DIET! Didn't he know stuff like that didn't happen in real life?

Uh-uh. Real life was much more fantastic.

One of the boys knocked the peaceful night watchman on the back of the head, making sure he'd be peaceful for hours to come. The Joker ordered the rest of the gang to follow.

Somebody turned on the lights, and the boys got to work. They started up the generators, climbed into the cabs of the parade floats, and quickly began to inflate the pitifully withered giant balloons.

No, this wasn't going to be a dull daytime parade. This parade was going to march down Broad Avenue in the middle of the night! His announcements had been playing on Gotham City television sets for hours—come see the parade! And make a few bucks besides! He expected quite a turnout, even at the witching hour. People always wanted something for nothing.

Too bad he'd forgotten to mention those other little dividends he intended to give the crowd as well. He was such an absentminded Joker! Ah, well. He was sure they'd all be very happy with their newfound wealth, in the few minutes they had left to enjoy it.

Generators growled to life, powering giant searchlights. The doors of the warehouse opened, and the trucks started for Broad Avenue, towing their searchlights and floats and giant balloons. The Joker's favorite float was the one with the throne and the giant banners that read "200"

The last of the trucks rumbled through the warehouse doors. The Joker waved at all of them. This was going to be the most perfect parade ever! And it was only the beginning.

"I'm prepared to rule the world!" he screamed.

Then he started to laugh and laugh. After tonight, he didn't think he would ever stop.

They lined Broad Avenue—first hundreds, then thousands of curious citizens, waiting for a midnight parade, and all that free cash. And the Joker wasn't about to disappoint them.

One of the searchlight trucks came first—a parade's no good unless you can see it, after all. Amplified rock music blasted from huge speakers mounted on either side of the light.

*Boom shakalakalaka. Boom shakalakalaka.*

The citizens—a trifle cautious before—started to get into the spirit of things. Some of them were dancing, others cheering. But all watched as the searchlight's beam focused on the leader of the parade, a giant balloon above them all, a fifty-foot-long cartoon clown leering contentedly at the crowd below. Then the truck towing the balloon turned the corner onto the parade route. The crowd gasped as they saw the float, full of historical figures—one of whom might of been John T. Gotham—and those wonderful banners: HAPPY BIRTHDAY, GOTHAM CITY!

How appropriate, the Joker thought, to have the birthday parade at night, when the real city came to life!

And there was more to come. A dozen floats, showing the finest details of this fair city. And the giant balloons!

*Boom shakalakalaka. Boom shakalakalaka.*

The citizens were having a good time now. And it was about to get even better!

That's when the money started to fall. The air was filled with thousands of dollar bills.

The citizens were amazed. But where was it all coming from?

Yes, there! Look up, in the middle of the swirling money, look carefully, citizens, at the float in the lead. There, in the middle of all the historical figures, including even John T. Gotham, was a throne. And on that throne was the Joker, surrounded by some of the best of his boys. Bob—good old Bob—handed the Joker bundles of dollar bills. The Joker pitched the bills up, up, and away, right into the path of a giant fan, conveniently located for maximum circulation.

*Boom shakalakalaka. Boom shakalakalaka.*

The greenbacks fell from the air. People realized that there was real money coming down. Now the citizens got really excited.

The amplified rock music had a vocal on now. The Joker sang along.

*Boom shakalakalaka. Boom shakalakalaka.*

This was the best! He had only one more thing he wanted to know.

Have you ever danced with the devil by the pale moonlight?

This time, he could ask all of Gotham City!

\* \* \*

"Welcome, everyone!" the Joker's amplified voice announced. "Enjoy yourselves. Open those hungry wallets!"

Vicki Vale couldn't believe what was happening here on the streets around Gotham Square. Corto Maltese, in the middle of a fire fight, was not as chaotic as what was going on in front of her. The crowd was pouring in from everywhere, people climbing over each other, trampling others underfoot, all grabbing for the money falling from the sky.

She kept back on the sidewalks, against the buildings, away from the worst of the melee, trying to get a few good shots for the *Globe*. She remembered what she thought, a few days ago, about the Joker wanting to start a war. Well, now the war was here, but the combatants were all of the people of Gotham City, fighting themselves.

A car horn blared behind her. Was the Joker after her again? She turned quickly, ready to run or fade into the crowd.

"Vicki!" It was only Allie Knox, calling to her from his car.

She jumped into the passenger seat. Allie looked over at her.

"You think Batman will show for this?"

Vicki looked out at the anarchy that reigned across Broad Avenue.

"He'll be here," she replied.

Knox nodded and grinned, like a young boy running through a playground. He started the car and drove slowly into the crowd.

\* \* \*

It was well after midnight. Most of the city was dark beneath him. But in the middle of it all was a streak of blazing light.

He banked the Batwing, sliding the aircraft between the skyscrapers. He'd have to land on Broad Avenue.

That's where the Joker would be waiting.

Knox's car had pushed through the crowds to the end of the parade. Vicki leaned from the window, taking pictures of the madness.

"Look at that!" Allie yelled.

Vicki looked around. He was pointing straight ahead, where one of the floats had jumped the sidewalk and crashed into a lamppost, bringing it to a stop. People swarmed over the float, fighting with the Joker's goons as they grabbed for the floating dollar bills.

Vicki started snapping pictures through the front windshield.

"Pull over," she instructed.

Knox eased his car to the side of Broad Avenue—not that, in this crowd, it made much of a difference where they left it.

Allie whistled. "Man, this is sick!"

Vicki tried to open the door against the press of the mob. She wanted to get a better angle on what was happening in front of them. She'd have to stay close to the car, though, or she'd get swept away by the crush of people.

"A girl could get hurt in a place like this!" Allie yelled as she pushed herself from the car. She leaned back against the fender, letting the crowd go by. She looked above the damaged float, up to a gigantic balloon that bobbed and weaved above the crowd. She took a quick photo, then reached into her camera bag for a telephoto lens.

She rapidly changed lenses and tilted the camera up to get a closer shot of the balloon. She noticed something else up there besides the balloon in the searchlight's glare—something green—as she focused the lens. It was like smoke, leaking from one of a number of large metal cylinders attached to the underside of the balloon—a cylinder that must have crashed against a building when the float went up on the sidewalk.

Smoke, she thought, or gas. The heavy green cloud drifted down toward the crowd.

She looked down at the Joker's henchmen on the float. They saw the cloud, too, and quickly donned gas masks. So she was right! Some of the other people on the float weren't so lucky. She looked back through her telephoto and saw a couple of them gasping for air. One of them collapsed onto the float, his mouth twisted into a rictus grin.

It was gas, then, made from the same chemicals the Joker had used to sabotage all the prepared foods and beauty aids. What did he call it?

Smylex!

The deadly green gas settled over the float, then spread through the crowd toward Vicki.

"Those balloons are full of Smylex gas!" she yelled in at Knox. "He's going to kill everybody!"

Allie leaned over and forced open the door on the passenger side. He held his hand out to Vicki. Some of the crowd in front of them realized there was something wrong. They started to panic, pressing into the other half of the mob still trying to reach the floating money.

"Get in!" he screamed over the crowd noise. "Close the door!"

There was a noise overhead like a jet engine, even louder than the crowd. She looked up. Some sort of black aircraft blotted out the moon.

Vicki stuck her head in the door.

"We've got to cut those balloons loose!" She took a deep breath, trying to quell the panic she now felt rising in herself. "I think I saw Batman. We've got to warn him!"

Knox grabbed Vicki's shoulder and pulled her the rest of the way into the car. She leaned back in the passenger seat, trying hard not to hyperventilate. He leaned over her and slammed the car door.

"Don't move," he told Vicki.

He jumped out on the driver's side.

"Allie!" Vicki began. What was he doing? He'd get himself killed.

He ran quickly around to the trunk and pulled out a toolbox. Vicki realized he hadn't used the key to open the back—the car was still running with the key in the ignition. This old rattletrap of Knox's probably didn't even have a lock in the back. He lugged the toolbox up past the driver's seat and placed it on the hood of the car. He grinned at Vicki as he opened the box. She could hear tools clatter as he rummaged around inside.

"What are you doing?" she demanded.

He tied a white antidust mask over his face, then picked

up a wicked-looking pair of wire cutters. Vicki started to open the door.

"Stay here!" he yelled at her through the mask. "Let me do this one thing!"

Vicki let her hand fall from the door handle. The panic had exhausted her completely. There was no way she could move fast enough to stop Allie from doing whatever he damned well pleased.

The closest part of the crowd had stampeded out of the way, leaving a clear path to the float. Allie tossed the toolbox into the backseat and ran toward the spreading gas.

"Allie, please—be careful," she called.

Knox rushed to the float, dodging those people still fighting for the money or struggling with the effects of the gas. The Joker's men were busy kicking bodies out of the way. Nobody noticed Knox as he leapt up between the miniature re-creation of Gotham City Hall and the cathedral. He reached the corner of the float and started to work on one of the balloon's moorings. On the third try, he cut through the cable. Half of the balloon started to rise, lifting the deadly gas along with it.

That's when the Joker's men noticed him. Knox dodged the first hail of bullets, moving toward another of the moorings. Then someone shot from behind him. One of the bullets connected. Knox went down.

Vicki had had enough of this. The bullets had started her adrenaline flowing all over again. Nobody was going to be a dead hero when she was around. She jumped into the driver's seat and floored the accelerator.

The car screeched to a halt at the edge of the float where Knox quickly rose and dove for the hood.

Miraculously, for the few seconds this took, nobody shot at them.

The spell was broken by the time Vicki had regained the driver's seat. Bullets flew from everywhere. She stamped on the accelerator as the rear window shattered in a shower of bullets. The rear window on the passenger side went next.

She got the car around the corner, but the bullets had hit something vital. The engine died. She pulled the decimated machine up on the sidewalk, so the bulk of Gotham Cathedral was between them and the goons with the guns. Still, they could get picked off in a second if they stayed in the car. Vicki got out and cautiously walked around to the passenger side. There was no gunfire. They had made it far enough around the corner so that they could no longer see the float—and, more important, the gunmen on the float could no longer see them.

Knox groaned as he slid off the car hood. He tried to walk as she supported him, but his legs kept collapsing underneath him. There was blood flowing from his forehead.

Breathing heavily, blood streaming down his face, Knox looked up at her. He tried to grin.

"You were great, Allie," Vicki reassured him as she glanced cautiously out at the street. "But don't try any more heroics tonight."

Knox didn't answer her. She looked back down at him. He had passed out.

# C H A P T E R

## Seventeen

*Boom shakalakalaka. Boom shakalakalaka.*

The Joker tossed another bundle of dollar bills into the air.

"That's right, folks!" he screamed into his handy portable microphone. "Who can you trust? Me!" He threw even more bills aloft. "Me, I'm here handing out real money. And where is Batman? He's at home—washing his tights!"

His laughter was cut short by a loud whooshing sound overhead. He looked up above the parade route. There, illuminated by the sweeping searchlights, was some sort of private jet, painted jet black and built to look like the wing of a bat!

Batman did have such nice toys! The Joker leapt up and down and waved.

"Ah!" he screamed into the microphone. "Wing-ed battle flies through the night, and finds me ready!"

He laughed even more loudly than before as he threw a final fistful of bills in front of the giant circulating fan. Now it was time to get down to business.

"Bob!" he yelled to his ever-present sidekick. Good old Bob. "Mask!"

Bob handed him the gas mask, standard World War II issue, except that it had thoughtfully been painted with purple, gold, and green Joker colors.

*Boom shakalakalaka. Boom shakalakalaka.*

"Hey!" a fellow asked angrily from the base of the float. "What is this stuff?"

Oh, dear. The fellow was upset because the green dye was coming off the money and getting all over his hands! Or maybe he was miffed because all the money underneath the dye was Joker money, with the Joker's handsome face right there on the one-dollar bill in place of dull old George Washington!

The man was still down there screaming, throwing the funny money back at the float. What did the fellow expect him to do, give away real greenbacks? Hey, the Joker might have been crazy, but he wasn't stupid! Nobody ever gave money away—at least nobody the Joker knew.

That fellow was a real troublemaker. Now he was getting other people in the mob out there to look at their money, and they were all getting upset! Cries of "Cheater!" and "This stuff is fake!" drifted in over the rock and roll.

*Boom shakalakalaka. Boom shakalakalaka.*

What could you do with a crowd like that?

Oh, well. The Joker guessed it was time to kill them all.

He spoke into his handy mike one more time:

"Now comes the part where I relieve you, the little people, of the burden of your failed and useless lives. But, as my plastic surgeon always said—when you gotta go, go with a *smile*!"

He reached beneath his throne and pulled out his handy remote control. He pointed the control up toward the balloons above, pressing the handy big red button at the control's center. The dozens of canisters started to release their deadly green gas into their respective balloons, making all the Saturday cartoon favorites bloat and extend themselves as they prepared to explode.

Bob—good old Bob—finally handed him a gas mask. The Joker screamed with laughter as he fitted the mask over his nose and mouth.

The balloons upstairs were getting more swollen by the instant, developing some unsightly bulges around the seams—seams that looked, temptingly, as if they might rip at any second. And when they ripped, that lovely Smylex gas would blossom forth—enough gas to cover half of Gotham City.

Oh dear, the Joker realized. He hadn't thought about what to do with the other half.

Citizens were starting to scream out there. At last, a few members of the crowd were getting it into their poor, dim brains. They were all going to die—and die in a very special way, with big, cheerful Smylex grins. Funny money fluttered to the ground as the mob trampled every which way.

It was hard to laugh when you were wearing a gas mask. But the Joker did his best.

* * *

Batman might never have seen the leaking gas if one of the guy wires on the balloon hadn't gotten loose. But, because one of the moorings was gone, the balloon was bobbing and weaving in an erratic fashion, caught in the wind-tunnel effect between Gotham City skyscrapers—almost as if it was waving to him.

It was enough of an oddity that he turned the Batwing around to investigate. A moment later, he had seen the green fog leaking from the metal egg strapped to the figure's stomach, and the Joker's henchmen wearing gas masks down below.

Smylex gas! It had to be. The Joker couldn't kill Gotham City with his subversion of household products, so he had decided to take a more direct approach. He probably had the gas pumped into all the balloons. Knowing the Joker, mixing the poison gas with helium might even make the Smylex more deadly.

But it was only deadly if it could reach the crowd below.

He was beyond the parade again in a matter of seconds. He pulled the Batwing into a tight loop, then dove for Broad Avenue, leveling out thirty feet above the street.

His computer told him what he needed to know. He flipped a pair of switches on the controls, one to angle the razor-sharp edge of the wings, the other to open a trap to catch the severed ropes and hold them fast.

He threw the Batwing forward, beneath the balloons.

The Joker couldn't believe it.

The Batman's plane was slicing through the wires that held the murderous balloons to the floats below, then carrying the balloons along in the jet's wake, a bright, bouncing, multicolored bunch of misplaced death. What was he going to do—let them out over the ocean?

"My balloons!" the Joker screamed. "Those are *my balloons*!"

The Batman didn't answer him.

Sometimes, the Joker decided, the other guy's toys went too far.

He was going to crash.

That was his first thought when he looked back out of the nose of the plane and saw the ruin of Gotham Cathedral looming before him. He had been paying too much attention to the balloon gathering, and now the end of Broad Avenue was coming up fast.

He lifted the nose as quickly as he dared. The Batwing responded quickly, but the cathedral was still coming up too fast. One of the wings would catch the crumbling tower. The engine screamed as he banked the plane sharply right. Somehow, he missed the cathedral tower by inches.

But the maneuver was not without its cost. The Batwing was climbing full-out, G-forces pushing Batman back into his seat. He fought against the pressure, pushing against air that suddenly seemed to weigh a hundred pounds per square inch. He let out a groan as he reached the control panel and moved his hand, slowly, carefully, down to the release switch. He pressed it at last, and the balloons were free.

Once his cargo was gone, it was easy to level the plane out and turn it back toward the city. The balloons were still rising as they drifted out over the ocean. They wouldn't be a threat to anyone for a while. He radioed the coast guard to alert them of any potential danger. That done, he headed to Broad Avenue.

He wished, absently, that he might have a moment to catch his breath. But every moment he spent meant more innocent lives would be taken by the Joker.

It was time to finish this.

*Boom shakalakalaka. Boom shakalakalaka.*

The blaring rock music echoed hollowly down Broad Avenue. Everyone was gone. They had all run away.

The Joker ripped off his gas mask and threw it down on the float.

"He stole my balloons!" he screamed.

Nobody had an answer for that. He shook his fists up at the sky.

"Why didn't somebody tell me he had one of those things?"

Still, nobody spoke. The Joker found this immensely unsatisfying.

He asked for Bob's gun and shot him. Good old Bob. That made him feel a little better.

Bob pitched from the float to the money-littered street below. He was quite dead. Good old Bob.

He stuck the gun back in his coat. It was good to make sure your aim was there every now and then. The other boys paused and watched him. It was time for orders.

"Wage war, you bastards!" he screamed.

He turned off the rock music.

Broad Avenue was suddenly silent, except for the sound of a distant jet.

* * *

He flew down the end of Broad Avenue. A few seconds from now, he'd be directly over the Joker and the rest of the human scum.

Batman flipped the proper switches to arm the Batwing. A computer voice softly announced when each of the devices was properly deployed.

"Searchlight.

"Laser gun.

"Gatling gun.

"Heat-seeking missiles."

That should be enough, at least for the first run. A few more switches and he had cleared the safety mechanisms and armed the rockets.

It was time for a little eradication.

Batman's plane was coming for them, low and slow. But this time it looked different, less sleek than before. It had things hanging from its lower fuselage, things that looked like guns and missiles.

The boys ran away.

"It's just cookin' good, you schmoes!" the Joker yelled at his retreating troops. "What's going on?"

The boys didn't even bother looking back. What kind of loyalty was that? And after he had made such a good example of Bob. The Joker hated to waste a good example.

A spotlight flashed on as the plane swooped overhead.

The Joker laughed, and danced out into the path of the onrushing light.

"Come to me," he screamed, "you gruesome son of a bitch!"

* * *

He was coming up to the parade.

Or what was left of the parade. The searchlights were stationary, the floats and trucks abandoned. Everyone was gone.

He placed the mobile missile sights over his eyes.

Not everyone was gone. In the magnified sights he saw a single figure standing in the middle of the street, jumping up and down and waving at the approaching plane.

It was the Joker. He had his arms outstretched, as if in greeting.

Well, Batman thought, if that's the way he wants it.

"Engage," he whispered softly. The computer did the rest.

Bullets, lasers, and missiles screamed down on Broad Avenue, all taking out their assigned targets. Batman wanted to make sure the Joker didn't have any more surprises hiding in any of his floats or other equipment. So the equipment had to be obliterated.

In the middle of all the destruction, he saw the Joker doing the waltz. Everything had missed him. So far.

All right! He was having fun now.

Things were exploding all over the place. There went a float, here a truck—oops! a building got it that time— bad shot.

Once in a while, a bullet came for him. But the Joker was faster.

A searchlight shattered, producing a magnificent rain of glass. The Joker had never seen such wonderful destruction. You had to hand it to Batman. This was what life was all about.

Unfortunately, all good things had to come to an end.

The Joker pulled out his other gun—the one with the real, real long muzzle. He took careful aim as the plane turned around for another pass.

He pulled the trigger.

Bang.

The Joker looked up from where the recoil had pushed him to the ground. It was a great gun, but it kicked like a mule.

Bingo!

Did he have the best aim anywhere, or what?

The left wing of Batman's plane had sprouted fire and a very satisfying thick, black smoke. The plane was wobbling badly before it swooped down overhead. The Joker ducked as it passed a dozen feet above the street. It was aimed straight for the steps of the Gotham Cathedral.

And that's exactly where it smashed.

There was a moment of silence before the Joker started to laugh.

# C H A P T E R

## Eighteen

Commissioner Gordon pulled his car over at the edge of the destruction. He could hardly recognize this stretch of Broad Avenue anymore. Windows and streetlights were smashed, twisted bits of metal littered the avenue and the sidewalks on either side—that is, where the road still existed. Up ahead, he could see the avenue abruptly stop at the lip of a crater. What had these guys been fighting with out here—heat-seeking missiles?

A dozen squad cars pulled up behind him. Gordon waved for them to stop. With the condition of Broad Avenue, they'd have to go the rest of the way on foot.

Mercifully, there were very few dead bodies in the rubble ahead. Maybe, Gordon thought, they could stop it before any more died.

This latest incident had broken Mayor Borg completely. He wouldn't talk to anyone anymore, except to mutter darkly, over and over, about "the death of Gotham City." With the mayor gone, Harvey Dent was running police headquarters, if not the entire city, virtually single-handedly. Gordon had volunteered to see what he could do on the streets.

There was no way they could have stopped the Joker's plan. His doctored coffee had affected over ninety percent of the force. So far, no one had died, but there were close to two thousand police officers hospitalized all over the city. And every crook and lowlife in town realized the cops had been decimated. Robbery and looting were everywhere—what few police were left could respond only to the most extreme of the calls. Dent had gotten the governor to call out the National Guard, but they couldn't be fully mobilized until the following morning.

A couple of the men had come to the parade on their own initiative, but the mob had been way beyond any sort of ordinary crowd control. Gordon had ordered his men to hold back until backup could arrive.

Now the reserves were here.

Gordon surveyed his troops. Fourteen cars in all—twenty-six men and women—virtually all that was left of the Gotham City Police Force. Gordon knew a few of them by name; others he probably hadn't seen again after their graduation from the police academy. They would all do whatever they could to keep Gotham City alive.

He had the twenty-six spread out across the street, weapons at the ready. He put a couple of the guys who'd brought their high-powered rifles at either end of the line to act as point guards, with the others following in a ragged V.

He led the way as they moved into the war zone.

"Thomas. I think someone is following us."

His mother's voice. They had just come from the theater. Why couldn't he remember the play?

The sound of running feet. His mother and father, so tall to either side, hustling him down the street, away from something.

But they couldn't get away. Not by running. He knew that now. How could he tell his mother and father not to run? Why didn't they know it?

They ran toward a man with a gun. A boy, really, only a few years older than he was. But the gun made him a big man.

The boy with the gun turned to look at them. Bruce remembered the smile. He had seen it so many times before. But the rest of the boy's face was different—made up like a clown; greasepaint white with bloodred lips and wild green hair. The clown was new. Bruce knew it didn't make any difference. They still couldn't run.

Why didn't his parents see? The gun went off twice before he could tell them, twin blossoms of flame that touched both his mother and father, turning them to ash.

The clown started to laugh, but Bruce knew he couldn't be afraid.

"Did you ever dance with the devil by the pale moonlight?" the clown asked.

But Bruce didn't cower. He didn't run. Instead, he walked toward the clown.

The dance was about to begin.

Then all was blackness.


What was it with these good citizens?

Here was the Joker, busy having a good laugh. And all these people started showing up from the side streets and bombed-out buildings. Worse than that, they had the temerity to be angry! Didn't they know this was the Joker's party? Heck, they should be happy just to be alive!

Why, the very thought of it made him want to laugh.

They didn't take kindly to that, either. They actually started throwing things at him. Imagine those ingrates! This was the last time he'd ever try to entertain citizens before he killed them.

A loose brick hit his shoulder. He looked beyond the crowd and saw even more people approaching, except these newcomers seemed to be wearing police uniforms. Perhaps, he considered, it was time for a change of scene. He should see what had happened to the Batman, after all. He was sure Batman would do no less for him.

The Joker pulled one of his smaller guns from his coat and fired a round into the air. The crowd of brick throwers hesitated in a most satisfying way, even backing away a bit. Much better. He turned and trotted toward Batman's plane.

Batman's plane exploded.

The Joker picked himself back up and dusted himself off. He certainly seemed to be getting tossed around tonight. Ah, well. You couldn't make an omelet without breaking a few heads.

Batman's plane had been a twisted wreck before. Now it was a flaming, twisted wreck. He guessed that meant a final showdown with Batman was out of the question. He'd have to have his final showdown with someone else.

He cha-chaed around the flames as he climbed the cathedral stairs, pausing at last to look at the burning wreckage. He was forgetting something. What was it? Who was it? Oh, yes, indeedy. It was a girl named Vicki.

Vicki came out of hiding when she heard the explosion.

It had taken her only a moment to examine Knox's wounds. The reporter had been incredibly lucky. A bullet had creased his shoulder, glass had cut his forehead, besides that he was unharmed. The two wounds had looked messy at first, but the bleeding had already stopped. He wouldn't die from either of them. He had probably passed out from shock more than anything else. She would have to get him to a hospital soon to get him cleaned up. But there was something else she had to do first.

She had seen the plane crash into the steps of the cathedral. The Batman's plane.

She had to find out what had happened to Bruce.

The wreck was a mess, all twisted metal and small fires. Nobody could have survived something like this, could they? She stood there on the steps, numb from the battle she had just survived. If there was any way she could find out if Bruce was still alive . . . somehow put out those fires, pull what was left of the plane apart. Vicki stared at the wreck and felt helpless.

The wreckage moved. A crumpled metal plate cluttered down the steps.

Batman stood in the remains of the plane.

For a moment, Vicki was dumbfounded. Then she started toward the wreckage—

She felt something hard and cold press her left temple. A gun barrel. The Joker's gun barrel. "Looks like I'll have to get you to the church on time," the Joker said in her ear.

He shoved her up the steps when they reached the entrance to the cathedral.

"Got to arrange for our ride," he told Vicki.

He took a walkie-talkie from his jacket pocket and thumbed the transmitter button. "Gotham City Cathedral, transportation for two," he said into the microphone. "Five minutes." He glanced up at the tower of the cathedral. Wow. That was one sucker of a tower. A lot of funny statues—gargoyles, they were called—near the top.

"Better make that ten," he said into his walkie-talkie.

Batman hauled himself from the smouldering ruins of the plane. He knew he was badly hurt. Pain stabbed his chest and he felt blood trickling down his cheek, under his mask, from a gash in his head. He looked down at his body and saw torn and bruised flesh under the shredded costume. But, he was still alive. He could still move. And his task was not yet finished.

He looked around. At the top of the steps, visible through the smoke from the plane, the Joker was entering the cathedral. He had someone with him, someone he was prodding with a revolver, a woman. Vicki. Batman stifled an urge to cry out, and began to run.

* * *

*Thomas. There's someone following us.*

He wrenched open the door to Gotham Cathedral.

Where were the Joker and Vicki? They must be some-where inside the ruined building. Or maybe in the tower.

*Thomas. There's someone.*

He shut the door behind him. There was a bar next to the door, a thick piece of oak, still firm. He placed the bar in the metal brackets on the inner part of the door so that no one else could come in to disturb them.

*Someone following us. But they couldn't run.*

He listened. There was no sound. The Joker was hiding.

He took a step forward into the rubble. There was a step down that he didn't see. He lost his footing, fell heavily into an old wooden pew. The bench fell forward, knocking over the next pew before it, and that the next pew before it, all the way to the front of the church. Like his own private game of dominoes.

The pews made a lot of noise. So much for surprise.

As the first pew fell, the Joker darted out from behind the altar, holding Vicki in front of him. They paused at a door at the rear of the church. The Joker waved and called, "Missed me!"

Then he pushed Vicki through the door.

Batman started forward. It was hard to walk, difficult to breathe. He'd done something to his side in the plane crash, then he made it worse when he knocked against the pews. Broken some ribs, most likely. He'd just have to hope there wasn't any internal bleeding. It couldn't be helped.

Couldn't be helped. Couldn't run anymore. *There was someone up ahead. A man with a gun.*

Batman found himself at the foot of a long, steep flight of steps leading to the tower, eight hundred feet above.

He began to climb.

Gordon and the police climbed the stairs to the cathedral. They had met no resistance on the way. The Joker, apparently, was on his own. As was the Batman.

The commissioner had seen the whole drama spread out before him. The Batman's plane, smashed on the steps of Gotham Cathedral; the Joker, firing his gun in the air to stun the crowd and make his escape; the explosion, and Batman rising from the wreckage.

Both Batman and the Joker had gone into the cathedral. Commissioner Gordon wondered what was going on inside that ruin right now. Part of him wanted to hold his men back and let the Batman take the Joker apart, piece by piece. Part of him, Gordon realized, wished that he could be the Batman.

But that wasn't Commissioner Gordon's job. Even if his instincts were right, the Batman was still working outside the law. And that sort of thing couldn't work, especially in a city the size of Gotham.

Maybe the city had lost law and order for a few hours. But law and order started again, here and now.

The door to the cathedral wouldn't open. It was bolted from the inside.

Gordon ordered his men to beat it down.

You couldn't keep a good crimefighter down.

It had surprised the Joker for a moment to see that costumed nut up and stumbling. But, once you had survived a dunking in toxic waste, nothing surprised you for long. Maybe the two of them would have their showdown after all. They would, that is, if the Joker couldn't get out of here fast enough.

But he had a date with a helicopter in another five minutes, and a whole slew of stairs to climb.

He heard Batman, grunting far below him. On the steps above him, Vicki was panting. The Joker himself wasn't breathing hard at all.

*He couldn't run. There was a man with a gun.*

There was more wrong with him than a few broken ribs. As the adrenaline drained from his body, he could feel where he had wrenched his right knee. He had to be careful to stand on it just the right way or his leg would give out on him. He must have torn something in his left hand as well. When he tried to straighten the last two fingers, he wanted to scream.

*There was a man with a gun. He knew the man's smile.*

He wanted to scream, but he didn't. He wouldn't give the Joker the pleasure of knowing his problems or his location.

*He knew the man's smile.*

The broken ribs dug into his side when he lifted his right leg. But he couldn't stop. The Joker was up there, somewhere, waiting for him. The Joker and Vicki.

There was a trapdoor overhead. The top of the stairs—and his ticket out of here! It just proved that if you kept a sunny attitude, any job would go right.

He reached past Vicki and pushed open the trapdoor. There!

"Upsy-daisy," he said to Vicki as he gave her a final shove up into the belfry.

As the Joker followed her up, someone said, "Hiya boss."

Three men were waiting for them—the three bozos he had hired from that Kung Fu studio. He had never learned their names, so that's how he thought of them—as Bozo One, Bozo Two and Bozo Three.

"What brings you here?" the Joker asked the bozos. "Getting religion?"

Bozo One, a lithe, medium-size man who wore trick boots, said, "I was getting confused down there."

"We come up to get a bird's eye view of what was goin' down," said Bozo Two, a slightly larger, heavier man.

Bozo Three, a huge black man whose face was covered with tribal scars, said nothing. The Joker thought of Bozo Three as the most dangerous of the lot.

"Well, well, how cozy, all of us together," the Joker said. "We have time for a little exploration."

He blinked to adjust his vision to the pale moonglow which was the only source of light and examined his surroundings. He was in a small room surrounded by four wooden slat-filled windows, designed to let the sound get out while keeping the rain away. There was also a pair of doors that led out to a walkway and the roof beyond—the perfect thing for a helicopter rescue. A good-sized bell was set in a rocker in the middle of the room and there were two smaller rockers to either side of that bell. Both were empty. Where were the bells?

The Joker almost stumbled over them as he turned around. They were *that* close to the trapdoor.

How convenient! Two bells so close to the edge—so close to a little accident!

The Joker giggled. You ever danced with the devil by the pale moonlight?

These bells were heavy suckers! He loosened one from its mount, with his acid squirting flower. The heavy iron rolled down quickly, smashing through the rotten wood as it went.

The Joker roared. This was even better than bowling!

Gordon barely got his men out of there in time.

The noise had been horrendous. The bell had come tumbling down the stairs, crashing and banging against wooden planks and stone walls, tearing away steps and mortar as it went. As it gained momentum, it crashed through a rotten section of the steps, ripping away a whole six-foot section.

By the time the bell had smashed on the stone floor at the base of the tower, it had done its damage. Maybe they could have gotten past that six-foot gap in the stairway, and two other, similar gaps Gordon could see higher up in the tower. But the rest of the staircase was no longer solid, either. Whole sections leaned crazily toward one wall or the other, and there were dozens of new holes and missing planks.

This stairway would never be used again. Batman and the Joker had the battle to themselves after all.

That was, Gordon thought, if both of them were still alive.

* * *

*Thomas. Thomas. Thomas.*

He heard his heart beat heavily in his chest. He'd barely dodged the bell.

*Thomas. Someone following. Can't run. Man with a gun.*

He was almost at the top of the stairs. If only he could ignore the pain. He closed his eyes.

*Can't run. Man with a gun.*

He forced his eyes opened and took the stairs, one, then another, and another. He rested for a moment on a window ledge. The stairs ended ahead at a closed trapdoor. Not far to go.

*Man with a gun.* He knew that smile.

Somehow, he was back on the stairs. Somehow, he reached the trapdoor. He pushed against it. It was stuck. He tried again, but he had no strength.

His eyes closed again.

*He knew that smile. You ever danced with the devil—*

"—by the pale moonlight?"

The Joker always found comfort in those words. Besides, he owed it to himself to say his little piece aloud. He had to have killed *somebody* with that bell.

He thought he heard a noise under the trapdoor.

He couldn't help himself. Blame it on a Joker's curiosity.

He pulled the second, heavy bell off the edge of the door and opened the trap.

There was nobody down there.

All right! Way to go!

"I must have belled the bat!" he yelled aloud with a laugh.

He was glad Vicki was there to share his triumph. Surely now she would appreciate him.

He looked toward the rafters. It was dark up there—the kind of place that never saw the light of day.

"There ain't any more of you up here, are there? Daddy or mommy bats?"

He turned to Vicki. "That was a joke. Why aren't you laughing?" He jabbed his gun barrel into her jaw and she winced in pain. "You're going to have to learn to laugh at my jokes!"

Light stabbed through the slats of the windows. Someone on the street had turned on spotlights. That was okay with the Joker. It would help his helicopter pilot.

"Boss," Bozo Two said, pointing to the trapdoor. "I think I heard something moving down there."

"Goody goody," the Joker giggled. "Our fun isn't over yet. We can play hide and seek. And whoever comes through the trapdoor is it."

On the third try, Batman managed to push open the trapdoor. Ignoring the agony throbbing through his body, he heaved himself up and into the belfry. He paused. He could see the glare of spotlights shining around the edges of slats in four small windows and, the shapes of two large bells and, coming from below, he heard sirens and voices. Gordon would be assembling his forces, searching for an avenue of attack. But, by the time he found one, whatever was going to happen would be finished.

Where was the Joker? Vicki? Batman looked away from the light to allow his vision to adjust to darkness.

Then he heard it—the mocking, insane voice: "It seems I have a bat in my belfry."

Almost immediately, there was another sound, a shriek, and from the gloom he sensed, rather than saw, something was hurling toward him. It was a man, cartwheeling across the floor. A beam of light gleamed briefly on two silvery blades jutting from the man's boots. Batman had no time to think, nor did he need any. For years, he had trained himself for moments like this—had trained himself simply to react.

The man reached the apex of his final somersault a foot above Batman's head and the blades arced toward Batman's face. Batman moved under the man's legs and his fist traveled in a straight, swift line from his hip to the man's crotch. As Batman stepped aside, the man howled, dropped to the floor clutching himself, and lay still.

So the Joker wasn't alone. How many others were there?

From the corner of his eye, he saw something move between the searchlights and the slatted windows. Someone was outside, on the roof. Through an open door, he saw the Joker with his arm locked onto Vicki's throat and a gun pressed to Vicki's temple. He stepped back, debating whether to rush the door or attempt to get behind his quarry.

He heard a rustle from the rafters ten feet over his head and, again without thinking, flung himself to the side. The bulk of a man dropped past him, the sleeve of the man's outstretched arm brushing Batman's cape. The attack became a plunge as the man continued to drop—through the open trap door and on down the stairwell. There was a thud, and a stifled moan, a moment's silence and then a final, echoing gong as the body hit the bell far below.

He started toward the open door.

Something blocked his way. A huge, hulking silhouette of a man. It stepped into the light from the window and Batman saw the face, a hideously scarred caricature of a human countenance. The scarred man was swinging a rope with a heavy steel pulley tied to one end—a weapon no less lethal for being improvised.

The scarred man swung the rope. As Batman ducked, the pulley passed within an inch of his cowl and, pain lanced his side making his gasp and, for a fraction of a second, lose consciousness. He backed away a step, two. A grin widened the scarred man's lips.

Batman backed off a third step and paused. His timing would have to be perfect; he might not get a second chance. The rope and pulley lashed out like a whip. Instead of ducking or dancing backward, Batman took a single stride forward, inside the arc of the rope, and drove the rigid fingers of his left hand into the nerve center of the scarred man's solar plexus. It was a strike that would instantly paralyze most human beings. The scarred man grunted, straightened, and his grin grew broader.

Outside, on the roof, the Joker hummed a Strauss melody as he waltzed with Vicki.

"I'd say we were made for each other—Beauty and the beast," he said. "Mind you, if anyone else ever calls you the beast, I'll rip their lungs out."

He laughed.

Behind the Joker, through the open doors, Vicki saw

the shadowy forms of Batman and the monster the Joker called Bozo Three. She knew Bruce—Batman—had to be injured, and probably exhausted. Could he possibly win? She thought she knew the answer, and for the first time, she felt a cold lump of despair growing within her.

Batman circled his opponent. His breath came in short gasps, and each gasp brought new pain. He had given the scarred man his best shot and it had accomplished nothing. How long could he continue before his legs would no longer support him? No more than a minute, surely. He scanned the belfry, searching for a weapon, but there was only the bell.

The bell!

Batman crouched, and sprang. His jump carried him to the top of the bell. For a second, he teetered, finding his balance. Then, as the scarred man began to whirl the pulley over his head, Batman leapt.

The scarred man scuttled aside.

Batman continued downward, past the scarred man and into the open trapdoor. Continued falling.

Vicki saw Batman vanish below the floor of the belfry. The lump of despair filled her whole being. But only for a second. She was alone? All right. If this had to be her fight, she accepted it.

She looked down at the street and the searchlights. This was her weapon—the fact that they were eight hundred feet above the pavement. The height and her courage, and her wits—these would be enough.

She gritted her teeth. And smiled up at the Joker. "You dance divinely," she purred.

The scarred man peered down the stairwell. He hadn't heard the caped fool land. It was so dark, impossible to see—

Two legs shot from the stairwell and clamped around the scarred man's head.

Batman had grabbed part of a broken rafter just under the trapdoor and hung there until the bulk of his enemy appeared in the opening, as he knew it would. Then he bent his body in an upward "V" and slammed his legs to either side of the scarred man's head. The pain was beyond anything he had ever imagined, but although he felt it, he somehow no longer cared about it.

He levered his legs past the lip of the trapdoor and rammed the scarred man's skull into the bell. Once. Twice. Again and again. The scarred man relaxed, went limp. His body slid into the opening and as Batman released it, plummeted into the stairwell.

Vicki pressed herself against the Joker.

"You say such beautiful things," she murmured.

Just keep him moving back, she told herself. Keep him moving toward the edge of the parapet.

She rubbed her cheek against his. "You're so strong . . . and I love purple—"

The Joker stopped, and his face stiffened.

Behind Vicki, someone said, "Pardon me. Have you ever danced with the devil in the pale moonlight?"

A gloved fist smashed into the Joker's jaw, knocking him away from Vicki, sending him into a sprawl through the doors and into the belfry. Batman brushed Vicki aside and followed the Joker. As the Joker was rising, Batman pivoted and kicked him into the bell.

Pain? Of course Batman felt pain. It seemed as though there had never been a time when he didn't. It didn't matter, not at all.

"I'm gonna kill you," he said.

"You crazy bastard," the Joker howled. "You made me! Remember? You dropped me into the acid. It was pretty hard to settle down after that! God knows I tried."

"I know you did."

Batman grapped the Joker's shoulders and swung him into the slats of the nearest window. The wood splintered and the Joker tumbled outside, onto the roof.

The Joker was clutching his mouth. He dropped his hand and a pair of false teeth clattered to the tiles and began hopping toward the Batman. For a moment, Batman stared at the toy, distracted.

The Joker punched him in the face.

Batman returned the blow. The Joker stumbled, but managed to remain standing.

"You murdered my parents," Batman said.

The Joker gaped. "What are you talking about?"

The Batman strode forward. "I made you—but you made me first."

"You lunatic," the Joker protested, backpedaling. Crimminie ditch! I say you made me, so you have to say I made you? How childish can you get?"

The Joker slumped and wiped at the blood dripping from his chin. He took a pair of black-rimmed glasses from a pocket and put them on.

"You wouldn't hit a man with glasses, would you?" he simpered.

Batman hit him.

The Joker flailed, shuddered as he glanced over his shoulder at the emptiness, and fell off the parapet.

Batman's knees buckled. Vicki rushed to him and held him until he could stand alone.

Then, together, they peered over the rim of the parapet.

Batman's knees buckled. Vicki rushed to him and held him until he could stand alone.

Then, together, they peered over the rim of the parapet.

Vicki saw nothing but empty pavement below, visible in the glare of the spotlights.

Batman glanced upward. In the circle of the moon, there was the silhouette of a helicopter descending.

Vicki gasped. Fingers had grasped her wrist and were pulling her. She had a second to see that Batman, too, was being tugged over the edge of the roof.

As they dropped, Batman's arm wrapped around her waist and, abruptly, she stopped falling.

Batman held Vicki in one hand. The other was stretched above his head, clutching the snout of a gargoyle.

The Joker stood on top of the grotesque statue, laughing.

"Grab something," Batman told Vicki.

She found a hold on one of the gargoyle's horns. Batman released her and reached for his utility belt.

The Joker stamped on his fingers.

Batman grabbed the Joker's ankle.

The gargoyle moved. A puff of masonry wafted from where the statue joined the wall of the cathedral.

The Joker pulled his ankle free and kicked Batman in the head.

A gust of wind tore at Batman and Vicki. It was the downdraft of the helicopter, now hovering directly over the belfry. The noise from its engine was deafening.

The gargoyle shifted, tilted.

The Joker extended a hand toward Vicki. She looked into Batman's face, asking a silent question.

"Do it," he shouted. "I can take care of myself."

Vicki grabbed the Joker's hand. It slipped off the end of his arm and Vicki's body swung outward. She began to fall, following the plastic hand toward the pavement. Batman caught her upper arm. She dangled over 800 feet of empty air, her hair whipping around her face.

The gargoyle tilted further.

A rope ladder popped from the belly of the helicopter and uncoiled down to the Joker. He grasped the bottom rung with his right hand and with his left fingers waggled a farewell wave at Vicki and Batman.

"Ta, ta," he called.

Vicki was again gripping the horn.

Batman saw the Joker step onto the ladder. The roar of the helicopter grew louder and the aircraft started to rise, carrying the Joker with it.

He had done his best, Batman told himself. Maybe he could get Vicki and himself to safety before the gargoyle finally tore completely loose and then he could rest. He had earned rest. He deserved it.

He remembered Thomas and Martha Wayne. Blood spilling onto a dirty sidewalk. The sobs of the child he had been. The years of loneliness.

The Joker was rising into the circle of the moon.

Have you ever danced with the devil in the pale moonlight?

The dance was not yet done.

Batman groped at his belt and found what he sought. He lifted the small gun and squeezed the trigger. A thin metal line shot out, up, and whipped around the Joker's ankles. Batman wrapped the near end of the line around the gargoyle's snout and secured it.

The Joker's eyes widened as he saw what was happening. He screamed, "Stop! Wait! Down! Down!"

His voice was lost in the roar of the engine.

His body stretched between the ladder and Batman's line.

Batman boosted Vicki onto the gargoyle and from there onto a ledge.

With a clatter of broken masonry, the gargoyle wrenched free of the wall and, like a pendulum, veered outward, hanging from the Joker's ankles. The helicopter dipped a few feet and, as the engine grew still louder, began to climb again.

The Joker's arms trembled with strain. Slowly, his fingers uncurled from the ladder.

For an instant, he seemed to be suspended in mid air.

Then, his lips split apart in a huge grin and he laughed. He shrieked with laughter as he plunged down, down, down.

The gargoyle shattered on the pavement and the laughter

stopped. But it echoed through the canyons of the city. It seemed to echo forever.

Vicki flattened herself against the wall of the cathedral, aware that Batman was beside her. Her eyes were squeezed shut. She could hear, but she didn't want to see.

She felt herself slipping.

"The ledge," Batman said. "It can't take our weight."

She was falling, her eyes still closed. It was funny, she thought. After all she had been through, after the enemy was destroyed, she was going to die anyway.

No!

Batman saw the street rushing up to meet him. To meet him and to shatter him as it had shattered the gargoyle. But he had time, maybe as much as two seconds, and that would have to be enough. If it wasn't, the Joker would have won.

He unsnapped his grappling hook from the back of his belt, under his cape, and with a flick of his wrist sent it shooting sideways. It clanked against one of the lower gargoyles. Batman circled his wrist twice around the wire attached to the hook. The steel tines scraped against the back of the gargoyle's head and sank into the soft stone.

Batman and Vicki jerked to a stop. The wire bit into the gauntlet of the Batman's glove and a wave of agony surged from his shoulder to his injured ribs. It was, he knew, the last new pain he would have to endure this night.

He and Vicki hung a couple of yards above the pavement. Gordon and his cops were running toward them.

Batman lowered Vicki to the ground and, a second later, was standing next to her.

It was over.

Wasn't it? Until this moment, Batman had not allowed himself the final proof. He had not seen the Joker's body.

Now he did. He gazed past the shards of the gargoyle to the mottle of red and green and white and purple splayed on the asphalt. He focused on the face, on the ferocious grin—a wide, mirthless slash of a smile that seemed to mock death itself.

"Over there," someone yelled.

Vicki turned to speak to Batman. He was gone.

# C H A P T E R

## Nineteen

Slowly, Vicki walked to where a crowd was gathered over a body, facedown, completely covered by the Batman's cape. Commissioner Gordon pushed his way through the curiosity seekers. Vicki followed his wake.

"Turn him over!" one of the onlookers yelled. "Now we'll see who this guy is!"

Vicki moved to the front of the crowd as a couple of them turned over the body. Gordon knelt next to it, shooing the curiosity seekers away.

The man groaned as Gordon pulled off his hood.

It was Alexander Knox. He blinked in the sudden light.

"Can I still make the late edition?" he asked.

This was the first press conference Gordon could remember looking forward to in a long, long time.

"All right," Dent began, "members of the press. Commissioner Gordon and I have a few announcements to make.''

He waited for the reporters gathered around the steps to City Hall to quiet down a bit before he continued.

"First of all, to clear up a little misunderstanding. *Gotham Globe* reporter Alexander Knox is not the Batman.''

The reporters all laughed at that. Knox, standing next to Gordon and Dent, touched his bandaged head in a mock salute.

"On the other hand," he remarked drily, "Batman is not Alexander Knox.''

Now it was Gordon's turn to say a word or two.

"Our police officers have recovered, and, although some of them have sworn off coffee, they're all back on duty.''

The reporters all laughed again. Finally, Gordon thought. This sort of event was a real pleasure, for himself and all of Gotham City.

It just proved you had to have faith. He had always told himself that if he waited long enough, he'd find something positive about his job.

Allie Knox was surprised to see a familiar, and very attractive, face next to him on the stage.

"Vicki?" he asked. "Are you covering this press conference?''

She smiled at him very sweetly.

"No," she said softly. "I'm going to disappear for a while.''

She leaned over and kissed him—really kissed him.

For the first time he could remember, Alexander Knox was at a loss for words.

"It was a ride, wasn't it, Allie?" Vicki said brightly as she turned to go. "See you around."

"Wait a minute!" Knox yelled. He couldn't let her go. Not after a kiss like that. "What about us?"

Vicki was already halfway down the street. Maybe, Knox realized, he needed a stronger argument.

"What about the Pulitzer Prize?" he added.

That made her turn around, at least.

"You get mine for me, Allie!" she shouted back.

But then she started walking again.

He jumped off the steps of City Hall, wincing when his head complained.

"What about your picture of the Batman?" he yelled.

"If he wants his picture taken," Vicki called back over his shoulder, "he knows where to find me."

She turned a corner and was out of sight. Another chapter closed in the life of Alexander Knox, ace reporter—another love lost before it could even start. He'd find it downright depressing if he didn't have the evening edition to fill.

He looked back up at Harvey Dent, who had taken over the microphone again.

"We received a letter from Batman this morning," Dent began as he pulled a folded piece of paper from his suit pocket. He read: " 'Gotham City's earned a rest from crime. But if the forces of evil should rise again to cast a shadow on the heart of the city, call me.' "

If the forces of evil should rise again to cast a shadow? How melodramatic could you get? Knox grinned. This was going to make great copy. The public loved this sort of thing.

"Question," he yelled out at the podium. He was, he realized, much more comfortable on this side of the press conference. "How do we call him?"

"He gave us a signal," Gordon replied. He walked over to the far end of the stairs, where they had rigged up a searchlight. Gordon turned it on. The beam, bright and yellow, shone on the side of Gotham Cathedral—a yellow moon surrounding the shape of a bat.

Well, Knox thought, the public was going to love this too. Vicki Vale might be gone, but the Batman wasn't.

Pulitzer Prize, here I come.


Vicki walked slowly through the city at sunset, a city that, somehow, felt much safer than it ever had before. Two small boys ran out of an alley, almost colliding with her. Both of the kids were wearing torn blankets behind them. Vicki realized they were supposed to be capes.

"Sorry, lady," one of the boys apologized. "We was playing Batman."

She watched them run away. It was nice kids could play like that again.

She heard a sound overhead, like a boot landing on cement. She looked up.

It was Batman.

A car pulled up at her side—a limousine. Alfred waved to her from the driver's seat.

"I thought champagne might be in order, ma'am," the butler suggested.

Vicki glanced up at the roof again. Batman was gone.

She got in the car. The bottle sat in an ice bucket, already opened for her.

"Mr. Wayne said to tell you he'd be a bit late," Alfred remarked.

Vicki poured herself some champagne. "I'm not surprised, Alfred," she replied. "I'm not surprised."

They turned off the Bat signal as the sun set over Gotham City, a much quieter Gotham City. Down on the streets, people laughed, music played, life went on. And overhead, the gargoyles watched silently from the old Gotham Cathedral. Long ago, it was believed that gargoyles could protect a place from evil.

One of the gargoyles moved.

It was the Batman.